MELANIE ASHFIELD

The Magic Orchard

Contents

The New House and its Mysterious Orchard

Just because people haven't seen something for themselves does not mean it cannot exist. Take magic for a start. Not the stuff you see on TV but real magic, magic that has been talked about since time began – that thousands of years of history and the cleverest people in the world still can't explain. Real magic still exists, it's just a little harder to find that it used to be.

Many years ago, before cities and towns existed magic thrived everywhere, in the fields, the trees and skies. People came and lived alongside it and humans and magic folk accepted each other and did not feel the need to challenge or test one another.

Then the humans began to grow in their numbers. They needed the space in the fields and woods for their homes, they needed to chop down the trees and they needed the space in the sky. The magic folk and their way of life did not grow – but knowing how few they were in number, compared to the humans, and seeing how the humans needed so much of the space in order to survive, they chose to take up less of it and live more discreetly. So, you see, it is still there, tucked away in untouched woodlands and fields, but very few will ever stumble upon it. This is the story of how four lucky children discovered

1

the magic one summer and what happened to them.

It all started when Sabe and his mother moved to a new town and his life began to change rapidly. Before that move it had always been just the two of them for as long as he could remember. They were not rich, but nor were they poor and they were content with no need for anyone else. The new house was the icing on the cake for them. That first year Orchard House was old, cold and needed a lot of work to make it into a home but it was also huge and beautiful with plenty of space for a young boy to spend many happy hours, exploring, imagining and playing to his heart's content.

The gardens at Orchard House were enormous and perfect for den making. Backing onto the gardens was an old stone wall, half crumbling away with a rusting iron gate in the centre which led to the orchard itself. The place was so overgrown and unexplored that it soon became Sabe's favorite place. He fought through trailing vines and flattened the blackberry brambles with his toy sword until he had fashioned a series of paths which became his own maze. He discovered the apple trees that had been hidden under the overgrowth for many years and wasted no time in climbing as high as he could and looking down at the town like he was its king from one of the huge branches.

One day he was exploring at ground level and attempting to make a bug hotel when he came across a rather large opening in a bank between the trees. Partly obscured by long grass it was too large to be a rabbit hole or badger set and he looked closer to investigate. It was big enough for a person to walk into if they stooped a little and then the tunnel seemed to head steeply downwards, although he was too afraid to go any further. At first he decided it was best to leave it alone in case he fell in and couldn't get out, but each time he visited the orchard he

2

got a little bit braver and eventually started to take a torch so he could peer below to try and work out what it was.

He was relieved to see that it wasn't a drain but baffled by how clean the passageway appeared which ruled out that any animal could have burrowed down there. He couldn't see where it led to but as he listened carefully he could hear what sounded like a river, gently swishing far below, and the faint sound of splashing. It reminded him of the sounds of a crowded beach on a summer's day. He could hear distant happy voices and water and hazy but unfamiliar music. Or was his imagination just overactive? Still, he was too afraid to go further. He spent a lot of time that summer wondering what it could be, but then the school term and colder weather descended and for a while

3

it was forgotten about.

By the second summer that they lived there, Orchard House was still old, still sometimes cold, and still needed work, but there was some progress on the inside. Sabe now had his own room and it was decorated and carpeted with space for all his toys and books and he was truly happy. His mother was happy too. Although he had not seen it coming, she had met a man called Jay whom she seemed to like a lot. He had a van full of DIY tools, and he was spending more and more time at Orchard House, helping with some of the work it needed. This meant that he was probably going to stick around. He also had his own three children some weekends, a boy and two girls who were close in age to Sabe and sometimes they would have play days at the house or go out on what his mother soon began to call 'family days'.

Ben, the oldest at eleven, was obsessed with gaming and flitted between acting older than his years and having no time for Sabe or his own two sisters, to wanting to join in with whatever they were doing as if he wasn't quite decided whether to remain a child or to try and be a grown-up. Amy was nine and a year older than Sabe; less impulsive and prone to deep thinking and role play games so that Orchard House was one day a school and the next a giant's lair. Megan, at seven and a half was the youngest and also the greatest lover of sugar Sabe had ever met, besides himself. She would try to boss him about so sometimes they were friends and sometimes he did his best to ignore her. He didn't know what they thought of him but he hoped he could one day tell them about the orchard, without them thinking him silly or that he was making things up. Before he had time to really think over how his life was changing his mother and Jay were talking about getting married in the future and how perhaps the children should spend a whole summer together. It was then that Sabe knew that Orchard House, and his life as he knew it, was about to get a lot more eventful. As it happens it did in more ways than one.

'Will I always have to share my toys with them mum?' asked Sabe as he remembered how the other three children liked to explore his room and whatever games he had set up in there. He was starting to get a bit worried. He liked his toys and games very much and didn't like the thought of them getting handled or possibly ruined by three other pairs of hands. Sabe's mother saw he was deep in thought and tried to reassure him.

'The children will bring lots of their own toys down for the summer and soon they will have their own rooms here too so please try not to worry. It will be very different to when they only come for the day.'

Sabe really hoped so. He went to find Jay who was busy painting one of the many empty bedrooms and asked him lots of questions about what they would be doing all summer with three new children in the house.

'I reckon you will be playing out most of the time, not cooped up in here. If the weather is good I can set up some tents for you all in the garden. Would you like that?' Sabe nodded enthusiastically. He liked the thought of camping in the garden and exploring the outdoors with three companions, much more fun that doing it on his own. He thought he could show them the orchard and they could find out what the mysterious passageway was and where it led to. He was suddenly rather excited about the children coming to stay.

Ben, Amy and Megan arrived at the house the first Saturday of the school summer holidays. It had been an exceptionally boring three hour car journey down south, made all the more trying after Megan had been travel sick into a McDonald's bag. There was also the knowledge that even though their dad would be there they were venturing into the unknown. They had rarely ever left the small village they called home for more than a day or two and the prospect of going to stay all summer in an unfamiliar house, in a strange town with two people they had only recently met, was starting to make them all a bit nervous.

Amy looked at the rows of grey houses with their uniform windows like hundreds of pairs of eyes and felt her stomach lurch. She hoped that she wasn't about to follow Megan's example. She looked at Ben, for reassurance, but he was just staring ahead, counting the minutes no doubt to when he could get re acquainted with his X-box which seemed be permanently attached to him these days.

'Does dad have WiFi at the house?' piped up Ben anxiously, 'Because last time he didn't have any.' The children's mother was concentrating on the road, looking for the turning that would take them from the busy town centre, with its swarming cars and many traffic lights, towards the suburbs where Orchard House was located.

'I don't know if they have WiFi yet Ben,' she said trying to remain calm even though she knew Ben's verbal protest was about to dominate the conversation. She was right.

'Well are they getting it soon?' he asked, his voice was beginning to raise and sound panicked. 'I can't do more than a day with nothing to do. If they don't have WiFi by tomorrow night can you pick me up?' he asked hopefully and looked at her. Was she laughing at him? Had she even remembered to pack the X-box?

'You will have loads to do all summer, don't worry. Dad and

Mel have arranged lots of fun days out and you are going to be able to camp out in the gardens, I hear they're huge. You won't even have time to think about WiFi with all the time you will get to spend outdoors.' She glanced at him hoping for a little enthusiasm.

'But I don't like the outdoors unless it's for football!' he protested 'Playing outside is what people did before WiFi. Can you call dad and ask him when it's being installed because I don't want a boring old summer.' He slumped further into his seat and was disappointed that no one else in the car seemed to share his concerns. Amy was staring out of the window and daydreaming. Megan had recovered from her bout of sickness and was happily munching her way thought the contents of a pack of sweets from the service station. Ben hoped that perhaps Sabe would help him persuade the adults to hurry up and get the important things sorted out . He knew Sabe enjoyed playing on the X-box with him and was sure he would prefer doing more of that rather than sitting in a tent. Amy gave Ben a reassuring smile despite her own concerns.

'Dad promised it will be fun remember? He grew up here and said he had the best childhood ever and he played out all the time. Besides, if it was boring he wouldn't have chosen to move back here would he?' she said. Ben looked thoughtful.

Amy hoped a summer with Sabe and his mother, Mel, would be fun, but more than that she hoped the summer would be eventful for everyone. But could it be? Would there really be enough exciting places to visit and explore? Or would it be just be grey and boring with not a field in sight like some of the people in the village said it would be (they had overheard a neighbour tell their own mother in the shop that she herself had been out of their village once to attend a wedding and she was knowledgeable about places such as towns. She insisted she had no idea why anyone would want to live in one. The air was bad and there was nothing to do.)

When they arrived, Dad was there to meet them and the children were relieved to see he hadn't changed a bit since last time. They were not sure what changes they had been worried about. So far they had never heard of divorcing men growing an extra head or set of arms but everything here was just so strange and new you could never be too certain.

There were shouts from their mother of 'don't swing Megan round she'll be sick again!' As the children stared in wonder at Orchard House she was going through a lengthy list of reminders for them. 'Don't forget to clean your teeth, call me if you get homesick, don't leave the chargers on overnight' etc. They were only half listening. They couldn't stop looking at the imposing house. They had been here before of course but only ever for the day and the prospect of staying for the whole summer now filled them with intrigue. Even Ben forgot about the WiFi problem-for a few minutes anyway. It was so different to anything they had seen in their village or through the car windows on the way here.

Obscured partly by crumbling stone walls and thick stone columns the house stood apart from new housing estates on either side of it. For some reason it had survived the bulldozers and the children felt sure it held secrets and adventures. This house and the whole summer was here, and they now couldn't wait! After they had said their goodbyes and waved as their mother's car drove away they were soon heading towards the front door. Their dad was pulling their cases alongside them and explaining that the house was a 'do-er-upper' and a 'listed building' which meant that it was very old and it couldn't be knocked down.

'Wait until you see the bedrooms I'm decorating for you,' he was telling them. 'You have one each, you should see the size if them!'

As they worked their way up the wide front garden through the overgrown grasses which lay either side of a winding gravel path the house loomed large before them. It had a grey stone front with spacious wooden windows either side of the door and all across the top. Overgrown untamed flowers spilled around the porch and front windows and there was visible splintering and a jagged hole in the door where it had given in to too many winters. They were going to replace it all soon, their dad was explaining but for now it was like the house that time forgot.

He wasn't wrong as they found out later. Although it had enormous rooms that echoed when you spoke loudly there were still no radiators, only real fireplaces. The carpets had been ripped out after being reduced to powder by the moths and there were only bare wooden boards and flagstones. To Ben's very obvious disappointment there was no WiFi which meant that he would indeed have a summer of boredom.

'When can you get it?' he asked panic stricken, looking to his dad for reassurance, his initial enthusiasm about the house quickly beginning to wane. The girls ran from room to room exploring and shouting about what they had found but Ben followed his dad around anxiously. If he could just tell him it would be this week he might just be prepared to try playing outside for a few days as long as he had something familiar to look forward to. His sisters enthusiastic shouting about how they could play hide and seek for hours seemed to drown out his voice. Finally, Amy and Megan clomped down the bare stairs to where their dad was trying to reassure Ben that everything was under control but Ben didn't sound very convinced.

'Dad where are we going to sleep?' asked Amy who had noticed the lack of furniture.

'I'll show you,' said their dad and he led them out through the kitchen to the back garden where Sabe was sitting happily in a tepee watching something on an ipad and his mother stopped hanging out washing and came over to them.

'Sabe, the children are here,' she called to him and he immediately jolted out of his viewing trance and the two of them came over to greet them.

The children studied each other awkwardly as children tend to do before they are completely at ease with each other but Sabe broke the silence and asked if they wanted to see the tepee.

'I've got lots of films we can watch in case you were wondering,' he said, and before long they were all sitting inside the tepee comparing notes on themselves and planning what they now knew would be a fun sleepover with the grown ups nicely out of the way in their own tent the other side of the garden.

Evening came and Jay and Mel made a barbecue on the patio and all they enjoyed hot dogs, chips and milkshakes in the warm garden, polished off with some home-made cakes, some of which they stashed away for a midnight feast in the tepee along with the sweets and pop they had bought at the services on the way down. When the adults finally went to their tent the four children stayed up late and Sabe told them all about what adventures could be found in and around the house.

Sabe described the local parks with their climbing frames and the ice-cream parlours they could visit; there was also an open-air pool called a lido they could go to if it got really hot and even a man-made beach with a bouncy castle that had appeared only last week and would stay for the duration of the summer. What intrigued them most was something he told them about the orchard at the back of the house.

Through the gap in the tepee door they could see the orchard was accessed by a small metal gate set into a lopsided ancient wall. It wasn't much of an orchard Sabe told them. The whole area was so overgrown that you could barely make out the fruit trees from the brambles. If you looked hard enough Sabe reckoned that there was a secret passageway set into the ground beneath the trees and if you listened carefully, you could hear noises floating about inside.

'What sort of noises?' asked Amy, fascinated and drawing closer to listen. The children were sat in a circle with their torches on, munching the last of the sweets.

'Probably builders,' said Ben, checking his phone for what seemed like the tenth time in as many minutes and hoping his mobile data didn't run out.

'Shut up Ben!' said Amy. *Trust big brothers to ruin things,* she thought. 'Ok, so there's no WiFi and we're not used to it but we're just going to have to find other things to do. What sort of noises Sabe? Tell us.'

Sabe lowered his voice and said very seriously, 'Sometimes you can hear water running like a stream, sometimes there is the faint sound of strange and magical music. Once, I even heard a whistle blowing and excited voices, but they weren't like human voices, they sounded smaller and more high pitched.'

'Maybe there's an underground rave going on,' said Ben, laughing. Sabe looked hurt and hoped Ben wasn't going to try and bully him all summer.

'Shut up, Ben!' shouted Megan and threw an empty pop can at her brother's head which immediately made him bad tempered and pinch her on the arm. He stomped off to his sleeping bag and moodily stared down at his mobile phone as Megan wailed loudly. The group dispersed as the adults came to diffuse the commotion.

Later when Ben had been made to sleep in the house and Megan was in the adult's tent, Amy opened the tepee door and looked out at the shadow of the orchard.

'Why haven't you tried to go down the secret passageway, then?' She hoped Sabe was still awake.

'I don't think I would be allowed,' he replied. 'Also what if I found something not very nice down there? What if I couldn't get back out?'

'Well, we could tie ourselves together with rope and attach it to one of the trees and then if it is not very nice at least we could come back? Shall we try it?'

Sabe smiled to himself in the dark. He had longed to explore the orchard since they had moved there but dared not do it alone.

'Yes I think we should.'

The Discovery of The Rainbow River

The next morning, after a full breakfast, Amy and Sabe decided to put their plan into action. They knew their parents would be busy stripping wallpaper in the house all day and so would have no objection to them spending the day outside exploring. They felt it was better not to involve Ben for their first visit as he was sceptical, and they would have invited Megan but decided it would be best if they distracted her so they could check the secret passageway out for themselves with as little interruption as possible. Megan however, had other ideas. She wanted to come along and said if there actually was magic in the orchard, she needed to see it right now.

They tried all morning to set up games for her. First, they tried hide and seek and tried to lose her when it was her turn to find them. The problem was that Megan tended to peep through her fingers and slowly creep after them when she was supposed to be counting so she was quite difficult to lose. Then they tried a bit of bribery, promising to bring her back a surprise gift if she stayed in the house or garden while they checked out the orchard but to no avail. She was absolutely insistent that she was not missing out. Reluctantly they agreed to let her come despite the fact that the only rope they found in the shed was quite short which meant that one person would have to stand at the top of the passage while the other one held it fast at the top. There was one condition; Megan should get changed into her best clothes just in case they did meet any fairies. Megan rushed gleefully off to the house and emerged quite a long time later in her princess outfit, sparkly shoes and silver tiara to find. Amy and Sabe were no where to be seen.

They had climbed over the crumbling stone wall that led to the orchard and traipsed through the long grasses and wildflowers until they found themselves so deep that the flowers seemed to be as tall as they were.

'Look at this,' called Amy. 'The daisies are the same size as me!' She stopped to look straight into the flower's round yellow centre. It looked like the type of velvet cushion her mother liked to bring back from her Saturday shopping trips.

'It must be a type of sunflower,' suggested Sabe. 'That would explain the size.' He had come to a standstill under a tree just ahead of her and Amy ran to catch him up although she couldn't fail to notice that the 'sunflowers' were now vivid blues, pinks and reds, and she knew they couldn't be sunflowers after all. Sabe was busy putting the rope round his waist. He crouched down and moved some trailing plants out of the way to reveal the entrance to a tunnel dug into a grass bank and some tree roots. He indicated that Amy should be quiet.

The children crouched at the entrance to the tunnel and listened. Sure enough, they could make out the distant noise of what sounded like merry-go-round music and splashing water.

'It's definitely not a drain then,' said Amy relieved. She had been worried that it might have been a manhole.

'I thought at first it was a giant rabbit hole but you can't get rabbit holes this size and anyway it's too clean. The walls look like they've been polished and look inside, there's lights down there.'

'Let me see.' Amy lay on her front and put her head into the tunnel. Beneath her, it wasn't dark and muddy like she was expecting but it looked like some kind of white cavern with wide ledges carved into the rocks on all sides. She couldn't see the ground but could just make out the glow of coloured lights that reminded her of a Christmas grotto. She looked up and it appeared the cavern extended upwards too, further than she could see, which was odd as outside the tunnel there was just a grass bank. From high above there were many swinging ropes made of vines and grasses twisted together and extending downwards.

'I don't think we will need that rope of ours after all,' she told Sabe. 'Shhh, someone's coming!' Sabe pulled her behind the tree.

There was the sound of high-pitched chatter approaching and the scuffling sounds on tiny feet. From behind the tree trunk, the children watched in astonishment as a procession of tiny people approached the passage entrance. They had never seen anything like it before. There were tiny women with elaborate hats made entirely of flowers and feathers and dresses made of layers of leaves. They carried acorn baskets laden with cakes and treats. There were tiny men with long beards and green tunics which looked like they were fashioned out of moss, and they strode in groups alongside the women, some of whom had hedgehogs on leads, and some carried backpacks heaving with miniature bottles of pop. Bringing up the rear, was another little person with wings poking out the back of their waistcoat. They were sounding a horn every now and again and with the blast of the horn, the parade of little people grew longer and wider as more of them came out from behind grass banks and dropped out of flower-heads eager to follow and join in the procession.

'We absolutely have to follow them!' said Sabe.

'Shh! Wait until they've gone. They might hear you' whispered Amy.

The children could almost hear their own hearts beating with excitement. After a few minutes when the crowd had all disappeared into the passageway and the noise of the horn and the chatter had floated away the children emerged.

Cautiously they climbed into the passageway and tugged on the swinging ropes to see if they would take their weight. They seemed very sturdy, and they decided to try swinging from one of them to try and reach a ledge on the other side.

'After all,' Amy said reassuringly. 'If we can swing from ledge to ledge to get down we can easily get out again the same way.'

One at a time they swung from one side of the tunnel to the other as the ground below them grew brighter and the sound of the music and water clearer.

Very soon they reached the ground, which was white rock like the walls, and found themselves standing next to a gently flowing river whose waters were so bright and clear it seemed impossible without the reflection of the sky. Along the bank of the river there were boats of different sizes, some were small empty wooden paddle boats with oars, some were bigger passenger boats with canopies. A large open boat like a gondola pulled gently alongside them, steered by a smartly dressed rabbit in a green velvet jacket and bow tie. He stood at the front of the boat holding a large oar which he stuck into the river to bring the boat to a standstill. 'Come along then, hop on!' he said to the astonished children.

They stepped onto the boat which rocked slightly and un-steadily until they sat on the bench in the centre and off they went-gliding down the bright blue river, lit on all sides by hanging lanterns fastened to the rocks.

'Fireflies,' said the rabbit. 'Cost us a fortune to install but we can't really run the riverboat service without them these days.'

They drifted past other boats, moored to the sides of the river and saw more rabbits in green jackets carrying bags and helping little people on and off the boats. Amy was astounded to see bright swarms of fish swimming alongside them. 'This is why we call it the Rainbow River,' the rabbit explained. Amy remembered something she had brought with her for safety. She reached inside her jacket.

'You brought Ben's phone with you!' whispered Sabe in shock. 'He will be looking for that and he's going to be really angry with us.' Amy was leaning over the side of the boat taking photos.

'I only brought it with us for in case something happens, besides I'll put it straight back in the tepee. He'll think he just lost it under yesterday's clothes or something.' She put it carefully back in her jacket, she really needed to preserve the battery in case of an emergency.

The river widened and branched off in parts, leading to other destinations. As they travelled further along it became busier with more rabbit-manned boats filled with passengers. Pixies with pointed ears and hats, mingled with gnomes with trailing beards and elves and fairies who seemed wisp-like next to them exchanged greetings and waved at each other from the various boats.

'It's a small community here, everyone knows everyone else. Are you visiting to observe the festivities today or are you on your way somewhere else?' asked the rabbit.

'We don't know,' said Amy totally in awe but at the same time terribly confused. Sabe nudged her in the ribs as if to stop her giving anything away.

'We're not part of the festivities,' he assured the rabbit. 'It does look like a fun day out but we're heading somewhere else today.'

It was Amy's turn to nudge him in the ribs.

'I wanted to see where the fairy people are going!' she whispered. She was so disappointed.

'I know,' whispered Sabe, 'but we will stand out too much. We need to go somewhere where we can blend in a bit more.' Amy had to agree he had a point, although she absolutely had to find out exactly what the festivities were later and join in with them if she could. For now, she had to be content to sail past what looked like a harbor where many boats were pulling up to dispatch the hordes of fairy people who were disembarking excitedly with their picnic baskets and musical instruments and heading in the same direction. She pointed out a fairy baby or two to Sabe, snuggled like small caterpillars on their parents' backpacks.

'The next stop is ours,' Sabe instructed the rabbit driver. The rabbit seemed to halt temporarily and turned to give him a quizzical expression. 'The next stop you say sir? Are you sure?'

'Oh yes,' said Sabe. He wasn't sure at all. In fact, he was starting to think that they should have got off at the last stop. They may have stood out like obvious strangers but at least they would have had a good time. It was too late now. He was going to have to pretend to at least know what he was doing and that they were supposed to be there, come what may.

Megan was furious as she stumbled through the long orchard grass tripping over her skirt. If there was a magic passageway, or indeed magic of any description, she deserved to see it. How dare they leave her out just because she was the youngest! Well, she would just have to find the way on her own and see what it was all about. That would show them!

She seemed to traipse about for a long time getting gradually more and more frustrated as she looked around every tree and among all the brambles and grasses, but she couldn't find what Sabe was on about. Eventually she became tearful with her efforts and sat down at the base of a large tree and began to cry. She was afraid that she was lost by now. The house seemed an awfully long way back and she couldn't see it for all the gigantic flowers getting in the way. She wasn't even sure which way the house was. She might be forced to spend the night out here alone if she was lost and the thought made her sob loudly.

The noise soon attracted attention. When she opened her eyes there were two crows silently studying her, their heads cocked to one side. She stopped crying at once.

Out of the long grass came a loud voice shouting 'I told you! I told you she was here and not there, but would you listen to me? No! Nobody ever listens to me! I'm just the carriage maker. Will you hurry up!'

Appearing from the grass was a large toad dressed in a suit and carrying a clipboard. Behind him, some small frogs were slowly dragging what looked like an elaborate gold box. As they drew closer Megan saw that it was a carriage. A beautiful gold carriage, with red velvet seats which they set down in front of her.

'Your majesty!' proclaimed the toad and the assembled wildlife all bowed. Megan really didn't know what to say.

'Now,' the toad instructed the crows 'Take her highness to the palace and make sure she is not late. This is the event of the year and my reputation as the greatest carriage maker in all these lands must be preserved.' He rushed around the carriage, polishing away splashes of mud and opened the door ready for Megan to take a seat which she was delighted to do. The crows then each took hold of the gold rope handles either side of the roof and Megan was lifted away and out of the orchard and up into the sky. She looked out of the window and saw the orchard and the surrounding fields and houses get smaller and smaller as she sped through the air.

Soon enough the clouds began to change colour from white to pink like candyfloss. Megan was sure they were actually candyfloss and tried to grab some of it, but they were starting to descend, and she couldn't quite reach. Down they floated, down and down, until she saw the domed roofs and turrets of a white palace. They landed softly in the gardens where the palace attendants rushed to open the door and escort Megan indoors. She could certainly get used to this treatment and wondered if they had any ice-cream.

Back at the river the rabbit dropped Amy and Sabe off at a place that could not have been more different to what they had just seen. It was quiet and deserted and they watched the boat sail slowly away with a twinge of regret. They looked and waited for another boat but there were no more boats to be seen. This was clearly not a very popular stopping place.

'What shall we do?' asked Sabe.

'We should just start walking,' suggested Amy 'Maybe we can find another way back to where all those people were.'

They began to walk. They seemed to have been dropped at a type of station, for as they walked out, there was a sign that said 'High Town' and then a signpost which pointed to 'High Hats Academy' to the right, 'The Old Square' to the left and 'The Village Centre' straight ahead. They chose the village centre in the hope they could ask someone how they could find their way home.

They soon found themselves in a little cobbled street with shops on each side. The buildings were rickety and old like the type they had seen on school trips and they seemed to lean towards each other slightly from opposite sides of the street. There were odd little people going about their shopping, but no one took much notice of the two children. The shops didn't have names, but it was easy to see what each one was for as their goods were displayed in their windows. They walked up and down, fascinated by the chemist with its 'cure all' spells and ointments. Coloured bottles of all shapes and sizes were piled in an elaborate display.

'Baldy's Delight, astonishing hair growth lotion. One squirt and you will have locks like Rapunzel,' read Amy and started to chuckle as she imagined half the dads she knew sprouting long princess tresses.

'Shrinking potion. Need to fit into last years' clothes? No problem! This will get you back to last year's size in minutes,' read Sabe.

'Look at this one! This is the funniest. Happy shots! Do you know someone grumpy? Do them a favour and put a happy shot in their tea. Watch them sing and pay everyone compliments all day. Imagine giving this to one of our teachers?'

A small, cross little man rushed out of the chemist shop and demanded to know what was so funny. 'If you don't want to buy anything, go away!' The children turned away smiling and looked in the other shop windows. Outside the bakers, Sabe was lucky enough to spot something shiny tucked between the cobbles and picked up a round gold coin. 'I'm getting hungry. Shall we see what this will buy us?'

It was hard to choose between the delicious-looking cakes in the baker's shop but eventually they selected some round shiny cakes that looked like enormous ring doughnuts, sprinkled with rainbow sweets. The baker, who looked rather bun like himself with his black twinkly eyes and round face, put them in a bag and asked if they wanted him to sprinkle some sugar in the doughnut holes. They said it was quite alright, there was no need, and they then went and sat outside on the wall and began to tuck in.

Try as they might the more they bit into the tempting doughnuts the more frustrating it became. Although they could feel them in their hands, every time they attempted to take a bite there was nothing there except air. A pixie-like child passed by with his parents and began to point and laugh at them and the shoppers who were nearby began to laugh too.

'I'm going to ask for our money back,' said Sabe. He had been very much looking forward to his cake and didn't like being ripped off. As he jumped off the wall someone commented,

'Look those children are trying to eat the bit around the hole,' and laughed out loud. Amy and Sabe stopped what they were

23

doing and looked at each other. 'I think we are supposed to eat the hole not the cake, as silly as it sounds. Let's try!'

Feeling a bit daft they discarded part of the cake and bit into the hole where they expected to find air as a small crowd watched them with amusement. They found themselves biting into some kind of invisible cake, as light as fairy dust. 'It's fizzy chocolate!' exclaimed Amy in amazement as she took another bite. 'I can taste raspberries too.'

'Mine is chocolate orange flavour, reported Sabe excitedly, 'and now I'm getting mint!' Every bite they took seemed to be a different flavour chocolate. It was the most wonderful and surprising cake they had ever tasted and they were disappointed to finish them.

'Fancy never having tasted a Chocolate Flight cake before,' remarked someone and the small crowd found this rather amusing as someone else said 'Where have you been growing up? Under a rock?'

Just then a van pulled up outside the bakers and some very stern, uniformed goblins stepped out with a huge net. The crowd dispersed and Amy and Sabe were left sitting on the wall baffled.

'There they are!' shouted the first Goblin gruffly. 'Playing truant no doubt. Back to school with both of you,' and before they could protest the children found themselves scooped up in the net and bundled into the back of the van. Suddenly they were being transported through the bumpy streets to whatever school the goblins mistakenly thought they had escaped from.

'Now we are really in a mess,' said Sabe as he rattled the door locks looking for a way of escape.

'It's no good trying to escape,' laughed the second goblin, who was racing the van through the streets, 'not even one of your escape spells will open those doors. The trouble with you witches and wizards is you think you know it all. You think you can just bunk off and no one will notice but we never miss a trick. Ah, here we are!' He slammed on the brakes and the van ground to a halt.

High Hat's Academy and the Rescue Mission

Back at the palace Megan had just ordered her third ice cream sundae of the afternoon. *I could really get used to this,* she thought, as one of the servants brought it to her with a little curtsy. She was sitting in the throne room whilst another servant was busy dressing her hair with diamonds, and others were parading various pieces of jewellery and coloured silks before her and asking which ones she would prefer her dresses to be made out of. She eventually selected a nice pale green and a white one with some silver diamond encrusted bangles.

She didn't have any idea why they had chosen her to be their queen but she wasn't about to complain. It wasn't every day she got to eat limitless ice cream and get new clothes. She wondered where Amy and Sabe had got to and whether they had found anything down that silly rabbit hole or drain or whatever it was. She couldn't wait to go home for tea and tell them how her day had been that was certain. How they would wish they had waited for her!

Amy and Sabe found themselves being marched into High Hat's Academy by the two goblins. The school looked like a very gloomy castle with dark windows and tall grey walls. Above the turrets, bats circled and they were marched through a large stone archway into a cold hall lit by candlelight. *What a horrible looking school,* the children thought to themselves.

'Suddenly mine doesn't seem quite so bad' said Sabe.

'Nor mine' said Amy sadly as she thought of the bright warm school building she attended back home. The door slammed behind them, and they were ushered up the large central staircase and into a cold room with high leaded windows. There were several long tables and benches set out with little cauldrons and textbooks in rows. At the front there was an old-fashioned blackboard and a teacher's desk. The walls around the room were piled high with books and glass jars and bottles. It was clearly some kind of science classroom. What struck them the most though, was the figure at the front of the classroom who had its back to them.

Clad from head to toe in an ill-fitting black jumper and trousers that were obviously too long was a child around the same age as them. Their hair was blond and stuck out at all angles like it hadn't seen a comb in a long time. In contrast to the neatness of the room the child was a picture of chaos. In front of them they had assembled piles of weeds; bottles and jars lying on their sides with the contents spilling out all over the table. On being disturbed, they now jumped in alarm and knocked over a cauldron which bounced and then rolled across the room, where it came to rest under the heavy boot of a goblin. The child grabbed the pointed hat from the seat next to them and hurriedly rearranged it onto their head. It slid down until it hung at a lopsided angle. They then gave an apologetic smile.

'Still catching up with work I see Marley,' said one of the goblins. 'We brought you some company. Two more defiant students who haven't earned their day pass. Now find a cauldron and get to work! You'll find the tests in the front of the textbooks. No one will be allowed to leave here until you've earned it!' With that the goblins stomped out of the room and slammed the door.

The children stood looking at Marley trying to work them

out. They seemed to be dressed like a witch or wizard but they didn't look at all comfortable. It was like they were in bad fancy dress. Marley removed the hat once more and tossed it back onto the chair.

'Never can get the thing to stay on' they explained. 'My classmates have pointy heads and ears which help those things stay put. My head isn't pointy enough and I only have one pointed ear, look.' They moved their hair back to show Amy and Sabe one pointed ear and the rounded one on the other side.

'Are you a boy or a girl?' asked Sabe. Amy nudged him in the ribs. 'That's so rude Sabe!' she whispered loudly.

'I'm Marley,' said the child, looking amused at what they seemed to think was a strange question.

'How old are you?' asked Amy

'I stopped counting after I turned one hundred,' replied Marley proudly. 'But I do have another birthday coming up soon. How about you?' The children looked at each other in astonishment. Marley certainly looked like a child but they had never heard of a child quite so old.

'Oh something like that,' said Amy. 'Is this your school?'

'It's Wizard High Hat's school. He's my uncle who has looked after me since I was little. He's training me up.'

'How long will that take?' asked Sabe.

'Well usually three years but it's taking me a bit longer. I've been a pupil for quite a long time, but I hope to graduate soon. Just need to brush up on a few basic skills.' Marley then began rummaging among the bottles on the desk as Amy and Sabe exchanged glances.

'Is Marley a he or a she though?' whispered Sabe.

'Call me he,' said Marley who had overheard. 'Just don't refer

29

to me as a boy or a girl ok? We have both at this school and I wouldn't want to be either.'

Sabe opened his mouth to ask another question and was stopped when he got another sharp jab in the ribs from Amy.

'What are they going on about, needing a pass to get out?'

'A day pass. It's Queen Augustine's coronation today. I'm surprised you don't know that. Practically the whole of our land is there. She's been away for many years touring her parents' kingdoms. In fact, many people have never had the chance to see her before but now she has come of age it's her time to rule.'

'Oh, and you didn't earn a day pass?'

'Well, no not yet but I only have a few spells to go. In fact. I was just finishing the one to summon a familiar.'

'What's a familiar?' asked Amy

'Oh you are silly aren't you?' teased Marley. 'A familiar is a witch's or wizard's animal companion, you know, like a black cat. Watch this.' Amy and Sabe sat down on the bench and observed Marley shake a test tube wave his hands about and mutter some strange words.

'*Hokaty, pokaty, fire and fur, show me the one with the magic purr,*

Flicker of moonlight, sneeze of bat, present to me my magic cat!',

He finished proudly and stood back, opened the test tube and looked triumphant as a swirl of purple smoke snaked its way out and down to the floor.

'Watch this, watch this!' cried Marley jumping about in excitement. They all watched as the smoke began to change colour and take on a round, solid shape, four sturdy legs began to form and a pair of pointed ears.

'It's a cat!' exclaimed Sabe 'It's blue!' exclaimed Amy

'Afternoon people I'm Tip,' said the cat. 'Right, where's my dinner? I'm starving.'

Marley shook his head, baffled. He looked embarrassed. 'Something must have gone wrong.' He double checked the text book. 'It's meant to be a black cat and it's not meant to talk. I don't understand.' He shook his head and reeled off the list of ingredients he had used. Amy looked over his shoulder, 'Sneeze of bat, black cohosh.' She picked up one of the bottles. 'Well, you used blue cohosh for a start. No wonder its blue.'

'Black cohosh, blue cohosh, same thing,' shrugged Marley.

'But it isn't really, is it?' said Amy as tactfully as she could.

Tip the cat, with her bright blue fur, was now being picked up by Sabe who thought she was rather cute even though Tip immediately remarked on what a silly looking wizard Sabe was and began laughing at him.

Marley looked like he was going to cry.

'I need to face up to it, I'm a useless wizard and I am never going to be free of this place!' He then sniffed loudly and wiped his nose on his hat.

There was a tap tap tap at the window and Marley went to open it. Two crows hopped in, and Tip immediately jumped out of Sabe's arms and asked the crows if they had any cake. She certainly wasn't a normal cat.

'Hello Marley!' said the crow. 'We thought you'd like some company and to know what's been happening over at the palace.' The crow cocked his head to one side. 'Your friends look a bit like you. Are they rubbish wizards too?' Marley was embarrassed.

'Leave him alone!' said Amy. 'He doesn't even want to be here, besides I reckon he's half human which is why he can't do magic.' The crow nudged his companion and lowered his voice.

'What did I tell you? We've been saying this for years.' Marley let out a sob. 'I will never be free of this horrible school, never!'

'Yes, you will Marley,' reassured Sabe. We are going to escape from this place and you are going to come with us. Over a hundred years is a ridiculous amount of time to spend at school!' Marley's eyes lit up. 'Really? I would love that. I can lead a normal life.'

'And don't forget me,' announced Tip. 'I've got my eye on a nice little cottage in one of the most exclusive parts of town.' She winked at Marley.

'You will never guess what has happened at the palace today!' exclaimed the other crow. 'Queen Augustine arrived to get ready for her coronation only to find an imposter had already taken her place! Imagine that. Someone was actually wearing her clothes and her jewellery, and she had eaten all the queen's special ice cream!'

'No!' laughed Marley 'Well who was it?'

'Well, this is the strange thing. She said she was the queen but then one of our magpie cousins found a gold necklace she'd left in the queen's new carriage, and it said *Megan*! Can you imagine the uproar that caused!'

Amy and Sabe looked at each other in shock. They suddenly realised Megan must have followed them into the orchard and they were very, very worried.

'Where is she now?' asked Amy horrified.

'Where she belongs of course, in the palace dungeons until after the festivities. Then she will be punished,' the crow chuckled.

'We must rescue her!' Sabe shouted 'Megan is our sister. Our parents will not be happy if we go home and have to explain she's in a dungeon. Everyone think quickly!'

They thought hard and eventually Marley located some old broomsticks in the cupboard. This seemed to be a promising solution until his attempts to make them fly failed. The crows then suggested that if they could make the broomsticks into seats like swings perhaps they could transport everyone in the same way they carried the queen's carriage.

Everyone set about tying what they could together until they had made the broomsticks into swings with sides made from shoelaces, and bits of rope and ribbon. The crows took the ends of these in their beaks, and they were ready to go.

They sat in a line on the broomstick, Amy and Sabe with Marley in between them with Tip on his lap. Up, up, up they went, at first bumping along the walls as they soared towards the high windows with Tip complaining that they were setting off her indigestion. It took a few goes before they could get the angle right to get the broomstick out of the window and the children kept falling off. The noise brought the goblins running back up the stairs to see what the commotion was about.

'Quickly!' shouted Marley. 'Don't let them catch us!' They heard the heavy key turn in the lock and the door was flung open just as the broomstick succeeded in sweeping smoothly out of the window and away into the sky. They waved at the goblins who were shouting all manner of threats at them.

'That was close!' said Amy relieved. 'Now we just need to rescue Megan and get home in time for dinner. I've had quite enough adventures for one day!'

The broomstick was gliding gracefully through the sky. It was better than any fairground ride they had ever been on. Before long they began their descent through some pink clouds. Amy couldn't resist holding her hand out to touch one and exclaimed with pleasure. 'Ooh it's candyfloss!' and she passed a handful to Tip who began to eat it gratefully. Every time they went passed a cloud, they competed to see who could pull off the most candyfloss and by the time the palace came into view their hands were quite sticky.

The twinkling domes of the palace roofs came into view. Outside in the grounds they could see a funfair and hear music. Hordes of people were picnicking in the grounds as they all awaited the arrival of the queen. In the centre of the lawn there stood a large stage with an elaborate gold throne for Queen Augustine.

'We know the back way,' the crows told them. 'If we hurry we can speak to the queen before she goes outside. You can explain the mix up and ask for Megan back.' They quickly parked the broomsticks at the back door and with the crows showing them the way they rushed through the back corridors of the palace to bargain with the queen.

Queen Augustine laughed out loud when she heard the children's pleas. She agreed that Megan's innocent mistake was the funniest thing she had heard in a while. However, she would absolutely not agree to free the prisoner. Megan would have to stay in the dungeon until she decided how best to punish her. However, she did promise to make sure she was fed well and would be given the occasional ice-cream sundae.

The children left the throne room heavy-hearted. They simply could not leave without Megan. They sat on the floor outside the room and tried to come up with a plan. It was no good. They had no money to try to bribe the queen with and had no idea where to locate the dungeon in the vast palace. Finally, Marley said:

'What do you normally do when you have a big problem?'

'That's easy,' said Amy. 'We ask our parents. In fact, I'm

going to try and phone them right now.' She reached into her jacket to locate Ben's phone. Of course, there was no reception in a land where WIFI had never existed. She stared at the phone hard and an idea suddenly came to her.

'Come back to see the queen with me. I've got a plan.'

Amy, Sabe and Marley marched back into the throne room where the queen, surrounded by her attendants was about to make her grand entrance in the grounds.

'Wait! Your highness!'

The queen turned around surprised. 'Hurry up then. I have a coronation ceremony to attend.'

Amy took a deep breath 'Behold this enchanted box!' She held out Ben's mobile phone to show the queen. 'It holds a rare and powerful magic. So powerful that it has the ability to trap anyone and anything inside it. I will let you have this if you will let the prisoner go!' The queen laughed again.

'No one inside my kingdom has magic that powerful. A nice try but you take me for a fool.' She turned her back on them.

'But look. I can prove it to you,' cried Amy. 'Look at all these trapped people.' She held the phone screen out to show the queen various videos her brother had made of him and his friends pranking each other. The queen looked in amazement and do did her attendants who were now gathered round in awe.

'You are right. It is powerful magic. But I have better things to do than watch little people perform in tiny boxes.' She gathered up her skirts and went to leave.

'But I have already trapped some of your kingdom, and if you do not release the prisoner, I will trap all of them, even you, and you will never rule.' Amy showed her the photos she had taken of the colourful fish in the Rainbow River. The queen gasped. Her face drained of colour and her hand flew to her throat. She then waved her hand at the children in dismissal.

'Very well. Release the prisoner!' she ordered her guards. 'She's eaten too much ice- cream and sweets anyway. I can't afford to keep her. Give me the magic box.' Amy handed over Ben's phone which the queen immediately tucked into her skirts. The children exchanged excited glances. The queen and her attendants left the room, and they heard the roars and cheers of the assembled crowds outside.

Megan didn't look too bad considering her ordeal. She had a bit of a tummy ache after overindulging and there was chocolate sauce all down her princess costume but she was glad to see Amy and Sabe. She was a bit surprised to see Marley and Tip but they were soon getting on well.

Tip said she was going to take Marley with her to visit some friends before they decided what to do next. One thing was for sure, Marley's school days were well and truly over. The crows escorted them back to the orchard in the queen's carriage and set them down gently near the gate to the house. They ran back quickly, expecting their parents to be very worried about their disappearance. Astonishingly, they were still stripping wallpaper where they had left them and it was nearly lunchtime, although they had been gone for the best part of the day. In the garden Ben was turning the tepee upside down looking for his phone but they assured him they had no idea where it was at that moment, which they later agreed had been sort of true.

Ben's Adventure

When Ben heard about his siblings' adventures, he thought it was the most far fetched story he had ever heard. The children had no immediate plans to return to the orchard as they were still talking non-stop about their first adventure, but after a day of having to listen to Ben accuse them of making things up, they knew they would have to prove the magic actually existed. So, after one morning which had consisted of a long argument between Ben, his sisters and Sabe, they were scrambling once more over the gate. They raced through the orchard again looking for the entrance to the secret passageway and promising Ben one of the best days out he would ever have. Ben followed slowly behind with his best 'couldn't care less' expression whilst whacking the long grass with a branch he had wrestled down from a nearby apple tree.

When they arrived excited and breathless at the grass verge where their adventure had started a few days before, the passageway was no-where to be seen. It was the most awful shock. Their previous footprints were still visible in the ground and there was a flattened patch of grass where the carriage had dropped them back but there was no tunnel to be seen anywhere. Sabe and the girls walked desperately around scrutinising every tree root and blade of grass and listening out for the faintest trace of music, but it was just an overgrown orchard with no secret and no magic, and the air was silent and still.

Ben laughed out loud. 'You lot are stupid. You make up a story about wizards and little magic people and you even blame them for taking my phone when we all know you lost it. Just admit it. You lied. I'm going home and telling Dad and Mel you've lost the plot.' Ben turned to walk back to the house, ignoring the protests of his siblings. They watched him walk away, swishing the stick from side to side as he strode with an air of annoyance about him, his outline becoming smaller and smaller and yet smaller still. The branch he was carrying began to loom large and heavy until it appeared to dwarf him. Amy remarked, 'I'm sure Ben is shrinking. He looks like an ant.' In the distance the figure of Ben certainly did seem to be reducing rapidly.

'Oh no, he's going to disappear! Something is happening. We'd better run after him!'

The children started to run after the dot on the horizon that was all they could see of Ben's head above the blades of grass. The branch he was carrying suddenly fell through the air and landed with a thud on the ground. There was no Ben to be seen. All they knew was that something very strange was happening and they had to try and warn him.

As they ran the long grass seemed to sway wildly around them, surrounding them until it swarmed above their heads. Pebbles and tree roots became huge boulders that they needed to clamber over. When they looked up to the ceiling of blue sky, the bright flower heads scattered in the orchard seemed to be floating upwards like multi-coloured clouds. Eventually they came to a standstill in what seemed to be a giant maze of grass and stalks. They had completely lost sight of Ben.

'Now what do we do? He's completely disappeared,' said Sabe and sat down on a giant leaf.

Amy and Megan's eyes widened 'Look at the size of that leaf!' Sabe looked down at the leaf. It was the size of a small boat.

'I want one!' said Megan and started looking enthusiastically around for a leaf of her own. She soon found one as tall as herself and lay on top of it 'Look at my leaf!' she called to the others. I'm taking this home and using it as a rug!' Amy couldn't find a leaf on the ground, so she began to tug at what looked like a giant red petal.

'Hey! What do you think you are doing!' called a gruff voice. 'You are pulling my wing off! I'm going to report you to the queen, you wicked fairy!' From behind the tall grass, a ladybird as big as the children emerged. Amy was still holding onto its wing in astonishment. She soon let go.

'I'm so sorry, I thought you were a flower or a leaf. I hope I haven't hurt you.'

'Hmmph,' said the ladybird. 'You nearly had my wing off, what were you playing at?'

'We were looking for the passageway that leads to the rain-bow river, then we lost our brother, Ben. You haven't seen him have you? He's got a football top on.'

'No. Haven't seen anyone,' replied the ladybird. 'You won't get to the river transport today anyway. It's closed for maintenance. You'll have to use your magic and fly back to whichever part of the land you came from. Good day to you.' He then walked off muttering, 'the anti-social behaviour of those fairy kids is getting worse. This would never have happened in my day.'

The children were stuck. They had no magical powers so could do nothing but wait and discuss where Ben could have got to, and how they would explain his disappearance to their parents. By this point Amy had managed to find a leaf and they were all lying on them, feeling the sun on their backs and coming up with theories as to Ben's disappearance. Perhaps like Megan he had been taken away and would magically re appear before teatime so their parents would be none the wiser. After a while a small group of ladybirds walked past them and remarked on what a nerve they had to still be loitering there.

'Be off with you! Go and make trouble somewhere else before we personally send you on your way!' shouted the ladybird whose wing Amy had tried to pull off earlier. The children immediately sat up and tried to protest that they weren't causing trouble and they had no magic to help them fly away. The ladybirds were having none of it.

'I'll get rid of them Percy!' volunteered the biggest ladybird as he strutted towards them. He began to blow the leaves they were sitting on. The other ladybirds joined in and the leaves began to rock so the children had to hold on to the sides to stop themselves being blown over. The wind around them began to pick up and suddenly all three of them lifted off the ground.

'To the palace!' chorused the ladybirds.

'Here we go again!' shouted Sabe, although instead of feeling scared, they were all happy and excited to be flying once more. They floated high up again, far above the grass and trees and it seemed the leaves knew where they were going. They waved at the group of ladybirds on the ground who were shouting at them not to come back, and they hoped the queen would deal with them.

'Friendly weren't they,' said Amy and laughed. 'Do you think we will end up at the palace again?' The leaves began to speed up and dipped slightly. The children could see the domed roofs

41

of the palace.

'No, we don't want to go there!' said Sabe quickly. 'I think when those ladybirds mentioned the palace, that started the magic that is taking us there. Let's all wish to go somewhere else. We've already been in trouble at the palace before. Wish to find Marley!'

They all wished aloud to find Marley and the leaves all immediately turned around and began to speed away from the palace.

'No, we need to find Ben first!' said Amy. 'Everyone wish to find Ben.' The leaves turned sharply to the right and began to descend. A few pink candyfloss clouds came into view, and they all grabbed what they could on their way down.

'I'm a bit fed up of candyfloss now,' said Megan 'I didn't have breakfast. I feel like some toast.' The leaves did a sharp left turn and swooped down suddenly coming to a stop in front of a very expensive looking restaurant with the name *'Toast'* written in shimmering letters across the front.

'Megan!' chorused Amy and Sabe. They tried making a few more wishes loudly in the hope that they might be able to float off again to find Ben or Marley, but whatever magic had been in the leaves had clearly run out.

'I'm starving!' called Megan, picking herself up off the leaf and rushing towards the door. The others followed unenthusi-astically. Megan rattled the door of the restaurant which was locked but the lights were on inside.

'Is anybody there?' called Megan through the letterbox. 'We're here for breakfast.'

The door was opened, and a harassed looking pixie beckoned them inside.

'I'm so glad you're here!' said the pixie. His face was flushed, and he held a broom in one hand.

'So are we!' said Megan. 'I can't wait. I'm starving. Where shall we go?'

'Out the back,' said the pixie ushering them towards the kitchens. You'll find the cleaner's cupboard and everything you need out there. Make sure the floors and every surface is sparkling. We've only got a few hours until we open and we're fully booked with a waiting list as usual. Right, I'm going to check on deliveries.' He handed the broom to Megan, walked out the back door and locked them in.

The children looked at each other in shock.

'He thought we were the cleaners,' said Amy in disappointment. Megan looked solemnly at the broom and then they all looked at the room they were in.

'Wow what a mess,' said Sabe. 'It's even worse than my bedroom.'

It really was. They were in some sort of cafe or restaurant which appeared to have just hosted a huge, out of control party. Elaborate chairs and silver tables stood on their sides, cups spilling leftover drinks of various bright colours were everywhere they looked. There were multi-coloured puddles all over the floor, some of which had congealed into sticky piles. Even stranger was what appeared to be clothing strewn everywhere, odd socks, odd shoes, jumpers turned inside out, there was even a pair of trousers hanging for some inexplicable reason from the ceiling chandelier.

'But why?' exclaimed Amy. 'Why would anyone do this? Look, is that the bar?' Megan walked towards where Amy was staring in astonishment. It certainly looked like a bar. Behind the counter were shelves of many untidy bottles and glasses running the length of the wall and floor to ceiling mirrors covered in fingerprints but there was paper too. So much paper scrunched up, scribbled on, turned into paper aeroplanes, and it was covering the surface of the bar and the floor. 'Have they not heard of a bin!' added Amy in disgust.

'Well, I don't see why I should clean this up!' shouted Megan, throwing the broom to the floor. 'I'm not a servant and we didn't make this mess; the people responsible for the mess should clean it up!'

'She's right,' said Sabe. 'We're not being paid to do this, so why should we? We have enough planned for today as it is' He picked up one of the pieces of paper from the bar and attempted to read it. He then laughed out loud. 'Guys listen to this,' he flattened the scrunched-up piece of paper onto the bar. The children gathered round to read it. It was a menu. 'Toast Celebrity Restaurant,' Sabe read out loud. 'Famous exclusive menu.' He stopped and scanned the food on offer. 'Well this sounds rubbish.'

The children began to read the menu together. "Toast á la butter, 5 gold pieces", "Toast á la jam, 7 gold pieces", "toast á la peanut, butter 10 gold pieces", what a rip off.'

'Someone didn't pay much attention in French class if they only know two words,' said Amy. 'Whatever next? Toast á la baked beans!'

"Toast á la baked beans" read Sabe. 'How did you guess?' and they all began to laugh. 'Oh hang on, there is something different here. "Chef's special...wait for it... Á la egg on toast".'

'Is that it? Is that what they think is an exclusive menu. What sort of idiot can only cook stuff on toast and pass it off as luxury food' said Megan.

'Sshh, someone's coming!' They heard a loud swooshing and roaring sound approaching outside like the propellers of a helicopter. 'Quick hide!' said Megan and they all dived behind the bar into a sea of scrunched up paper and discarded cups.

The key turned in the lock and they heard the voice of the pixie that had locked them in earlier.

'What on earth is going on here!' shouted another voice which was very loud and cross.

'We have our annual talent show this evening. Tickets to this restaurant are sold out! Every famous face in the county will be here. I need this mess sorting out immediately!' There was the scrunch of boots on the floor, the swish of a cape above the bar from who appeared to be the restaurant's owner.

'Yes sir, I'll see to it sir. The cleaners were here a moment ago. I can't think where they could have got to. I'm positive I locked them in.'

'I don't care if you have to clean it yourself!' boomed the voice. 'I will not have my reputation as the greatest and most famous chef that ever lived ruined by your incompetence do you hear? I'm set to make a lot of money here tonight and I have plans to expand.'

'Yes sir, of course sir.' The pixie sobbed and began to sweep up the mess with the broom.

The very cross owner began to stride towards the bar that the children were hiding behind, stomp, stomp stomp! A pair of gold boots and an elaborate fur cape swished towards them as the owner stood with his back to them to fix himself a drink, kicking paper and last night's rubbish out of his way as he went to fill his glass. Megan whispered loudly that he was rather small for a man. The owner turned around in surprise at hearing her voice and gasped when he saw the three children crouching on the floor. They in turn were astonished by the owner's appearance.

'Ben!' they all whispered in amazement.

'Sshh!' whispered Ben motioning for them to stay hidden. 'It's Sir Ben, by the way. I got a knighthood for services to the restaurant industry.'

'But your menu is terrible!' remarked Megan. Ben looked deeply offended. He crouched down to their level. 'My menu is actually the best in this land! Before I arrived, everyone here lived off grass and seeds and the occasional cake if they could afford it. My menu was revolutionary! My talents have brought me the sort of fame and wealth you can only dream about. Don't any of you ever describe my menu as terrible again. Now, will you please help with the cleaning. We have a really important talent show on tonight.'

'No' said Megan

'Do it yourself,' said Sabe.

'Toast a la peanut butter!' said Amy and they all started to giggle.

'Please be quiet. If you help me sort this place out and keep my reputation, I will do anything' He looked at them in desperation. Finally, Sabe spoke up.

'We are trying to find our friend Marley. We have some transport, but it seems to have run out of fuel. If you can find him for us, we'll keep your silly secret and help you clean up.'

Ben nodded his head. 'I don't know anyone of that name but I can get your transport moving again. I have some flying fuel out the back. I'll also give you VIP tickets for tonight. Come and enjoy the Toast experience. You won't regret it, just please don't blow my cover.'

Everyone agreed to help out. They couldn't wait to see Marley again. 'But Ben,' asked Amy. 'How long have you been here? You've only just left the orchard.'

'Well, I woke up here. I figured I'd fallen over in that silly overgrown Orchard and whacked my head on a tree or something. I thought it was concussion. Anyway I was hungry. I went looking for something to eat and could find nothing nice. I realised very quickly that there was a gap in the market here, so I made a few useful contacts and launched my flagship restaurant Toast. That was around a year ago. The rest is history.'

'A year?' whispered Megan before adding 'and I bet you still haven't changed your socks.'

Ben grabbed her by the back of her jumper and hauled her to

her feet.

'I believe I have just found our missing cleaners!' he announced to the flustered pixie.

After cleaning the restaurant from top to bottom the children were exhausted and glad to leave. Ben proudly gave them some toast with butter to thank them and they were so hungry they accepted it reluctantly. The pixie who managed the restaurant was baffled by their lack of enthusiasm for such a generous gesture and told them they were very fortunate. The children suggested that Sir Ben was the fortunate one to have such brilliant cleaning staff. Sir Ben emerged from the kitchens bearing an envelope.

'VIP tickets for tonight as promised, one for your friend Marley too.' Amy tucked them into her pocket. He also handed them a cannister of what he told them was flying fuel and told them to sprinkle it on anything that needed moving, say where they wanted to go, and the magic would do the rest.

Once outside they sprinkled a little of the cannister's contents onto the leaves they had arrived on and watched as the leaves began to bob and float above the ground.

'Quick jump on,' they shouted to each other and began to scramble onto each of their leaves and balance carefully in the middle, holding onto the sides as each leaf began to rise up into the air. Ben came outside to wave them off.

'Hope to see you later!' he shouted.

'Take us to see Marley' they chorused waving back to Ben as they flew away, picking up speed. Megan leaned over the side to call to Ben as she rode out of sight, 'And don't forget to change your socks!' delighted that he was too far away to do anything to get her back.

Off to Marley's Cottage

The children flew onwards. They could view the whole county from up here and it was a fascinating journey. One minute they were passing over pink and blue fields, the next they could see bright green woods and were pointing out some unusual looking birds flying between the trees. The land seemed to be split into distinctly different parts, each with its own character. One minute it was bright and colourful with rows of neat houses and fields, the next it was as dark as night with dense forests and hardly any signs of life.

'Isn't that High Hat's academy?' called Sabe, pointing to three black spiky towers outlined against a dark sky. The leaves began to descend towards the towers.

'No! No!' shouted the girls in panic. 'We don't want to go there! Take us to Marley!'

'Oh sorry I forgot how these things work,' said Sabe as the leaves floated upwards and over the top of the towers.

Leaving the gloomy shadow of the academy behind them, they emerged once more into a bright and sunny landscape and the leaves shortly began to descend towards a small white cottage with a thatched roof standing alone in a beautiful garden. They began to slow down and came to a soft landing on the lawn outside.

'Isn't it beautiful,' exclaimed Amy stepping off her leaf and looking round. 'It's like a house from a fairy-tale.'

'This must be Marley's house,' said Sabe. 'Shall we knock on the door and see?'

The children lifted the polished brass knocker and knocked hard on the door. After a while a very dishevelled and sad looking Marley answered. He looked like he had been crying. Amy gave him a big hug and the children crowded round him to ask what was wrong.

'Are you missing your school?' asked Sabe.

'No it's not that,' sniffed Marley and began to wipe his nose on his sleeve. 'I hated school. It's Tip. We had a row and she stormed out this morning. That cat drives me mad with her constant hovering around me but now I feel completely lost without her!' He began to sob. The children managed to coax Marley into the kitchen where he sat at the wooden table and dabbed his eyes on a tea towel.

The children looked round at kitchen. There was a mixing bowl on the worktop with remains of a cake mix inside. Megan wiped her fingers around the inside and began to lick the leftovers.

'This is yummy,' she remarked. There were balloons on the floor and more waiting to be blown up on another surface and next to these was a pile of sparkling, carefully wrapped presents.

'Whose birthday is it?' asked Sabe.

'It's mine,' said Marley sheepishly. 'I'm a hundred and something or other today. The thing is, I've never celebrated any of my birthdays. I don't even tell anyone when I have one, but Tip being a magic cat, of course she already knew and this is the problem. She got very excited and decided to take over. She insisted on the balloons, the cake, the presents, started talking about throwing a party for me. It just made me feel really worried and nervous. Then as if all that wasn't bad enough wait until you see the party outfit she ordered for me.' He opened a bag on the kitchen table and pulled out a smart blue shirt, jeans and a pair of trainers.

'What's wrong with those?' said Sabe. 'I would wear them.'

'It's not that there is anything wrong with them exactly' explained Marley 'It's just that she is trying to change me. If I become who she wants me to be then I won't know myself anymore. She has even tried to coax me into changing my hair. She actually put a spell on a pair of scissors and a comb and got them to follow me round. They even followed me to the bathroom just so I got the hint.'

The children looked at Marley's wild blonde hair. He did desperately need a haircut. His black trousers were faded at the knees and there were holes and loose threads in his school jumper.'

'I think Tip has a point actually,' said Megan 'You shouldn't still be wearing school uniform if you've run away from the academy. Why not let her buy you some new clothes?' Marley looked at her in alarm.

'But I don't want to change. I'm comfortable as I am. Besides, my uncle High Hat put spells on everyone's uniforms to make them self-washing. I don't ever have to get changed. He says it saves a fortune.' He stroked his cloak with pride.

'I wouldn't be very happy if I had to wear school uniform every day, even at weekends,' said Amy, shuddering at the thought.

'What's that smell?' called Megan from the kitchen counter where she was demolishing the remains of the cake mix.

Everyone looked round to see smoke starting to pour out of the oven door.

'That will be my birthday cake,' said Marley. 'Tip and I started it this morning. Do you think it's ready yet?'

'Ready?' shouted Amy, quickly running to turn the oven off. 'I should think it's like a bonfire by now!'

She grabbed some tea towels and eased the cake tin out of the oven whilst the air in the kitchen filled with smoke. Sabe opened a window. The cake was placed on the worktop. It was as black as coal.

'It will be fine,' said Marley unconvincingly. 'I'll just do a quick spell and sort out the damage. Then we can all have a slice. It looks like a meteorite, doesn't it? I always wanted a meteorite.'

The children exchanged worried glances. As much as they loved cake, they didn't think they could stand to even eat a mouthful of that burnt offering. Marley had started to chant. His hands were waving over the cake.

'*I summon the magic of Partyland! Send sugar and eggs and* erm...What else is in a cake?' he whispered to the children

'Flour and butter,' said Sabe

'And don't forget the icing,' added Megan.

'And the candles,' said Amy

'Maybe leave the candles,' suggested Sabe, trying to visualise over one hundred candles on a cake.

'*Partyland butter, icing and flour!*' continued Marley waving his arms determinedly.

'*Send me a cake and send it this hour.*
Create the best birthday cake ever seen,
with icing any colour except pink or green!'

It didn't sound like the most convincing spell but at once the cake began to rock from side to side, it rattled in its tin as if trying to escape. They all watched in fascination as the cake began to transform itself.

'It's working! It's working!' shouted Marley triumphantly. 'See I knew I could look after myself!' The cake began to rise and soon its hard, burnt exterior began to fade and soften.

'Oh, it's a cake! And it's starting to look delicious!' cried Megan.

Marley handed round plates. The children watched in amazement as the cake freed itself from its tin and floated over to the cake stand Tip had prepared that morning. Piping bags appeared in midair and began to decorate the cake in white and blue. The words, 'Happy Birthday Marley', were carefully written onto the top by an invisible hand and before long there was a perfect birthday cake sitting on the table ready to be eaten.

'That was brilliant Marley!' the children congratulated him, and Marley began to cut into the cake, ready to put onto plates for them all to enjoy. The knife he was holding had only just sliced through the thick icing when they heard a clunking sound as it came into contact with something hard.

'That's strange, said Marley and tried to cut the other side. The same thing happened. He broke a piece of icing off. Underneath it was obvious that it was the same cake that had come out of the oven, burned to a stubborn hard rock. Everyone's faces fell. They had been really looking forward to eating it.

'Well, my uncle always said I could only ever do a half job,' said Marley. He was clearly embarrassed and disappointed.

'Your uncle doesn't sound very nice if you ask me,' said Amy. 'Shall we think of something else to do for your birthday instead?'

'I don't know if I can even be bothered' said Marley. 'Based on what has happened so far I think birthdays are overrated'

'No, Marley, birthdays are brilliant,' Sabe told him. 'You get toys and other stuff you have wanted for ages, and you get your favourite food, a party with your friends, or a fun day out somewhere. Birthdays are really important, and you should have celebrated every single one of them.' Marley looked intrigued. 'That's what Tip said too, but Uncle High Hat said they were just another day and only empty-headed people and stupid wizards and witches celebrate birthdays.' The children were visibly shocked.

'Ok that's it!' said Sabe 'I've heard enough about this horrible uncle of yours. We are going to help you celebrate your birthday and hopefully Tip will come home soon and she can join in too. Where would you most like to go?' They all waited for an answer. Marley looked puzzled.

'Well, I suppose we could go for a walk. It's very pretty round here and Tip has some friends that live nearby. Sometimes we go for tea, and they talk about food and how the land used to be in the old days and I'm allowed to play in the gardens.'

'Is that it?' said Megan. 'Your free time makes you sound like an old person. We have seen more of this land than you have and this is only our second visit.'

'We could always take him to Toast restaurant' teased Amy. Marley's eyes suddenly opened very wide and he looked excited.

'I have heard of Toast!' he exclaimed 'Everyone has. But only the richest and most important people are allowed in. I've heard the food is very special, but I doubt we could get in. Even Tip's friends have been on the waiting list for ages.'

'Well look what I've got!' announced Amy, pulling the restaurant tickets triumphantly out of her pocket. Marley could not believe his eyes. He reached out to hold the tickets and regarded them in awe.

'But how did you get these? My name is even on one of them. It seems almost impossible.'

'Ah well we used our own magic,' said Amy and gave a look to Megan and Sabe which suggested that they were not to tell Marley the truth about Ben's restaurant and how they came to get the tickets.

That afternoon, having failed to persuade a very excited Marley to get changed into his birthday outfit, the children were ready to go back to Ben's restaurant. They had wondered whether to let Marley know that the Toast experience was a daily occurrence for them in their world and there were even better things to eat there but looking at him, as hyper as a new puppy, they decided not to dampen his enthusiasm by criticising the best restaurant the land had ever seen.

'We should open a pizza restaurant next time we come,' suggested Megan. 'Then we can make lots of money and be famous like Ben.'

'I don't know,' said Amy. 'I would get sick of it very quickly. 'There must be other ways of becoming famous here.'

'Marley says the winner of the talent show tonight will take home a treasure chest of gold pieces' said Sabe. 'Maybe we could enter. I could make up a rap or something.' The girls looked at him strangely.

'Let's just enjoy watching the show instead,' suggested Amy. 'It will be fun to see what the people who live round here can do. Besides, I don't think anyone would know what a rap is. They would think you were just casting an angry spell and we might get asked to leave.' Sabe looked thoughtful but felt she did have a point.

They decided that the flying leaves they had arrived on should stay in the garden. All afternoon they had been having great fun deciding what form of transport they could take together. They had plenty of flying fuel left in the can Ben had given them and carefully considered the merits of sprinkling it on various items of furniture in the cottage. The problem was most of the stuff that would fit all of them on probably wouldn't get through the front door. This ruled out the comfy sofa, the beds and the free-standing bath.

'What about the shed in the garden?' suggested Sabe after he had conducted a full search of the cottage and had found nothing suitable.

'Well, it would look really weird if we arrive in a flying shed, but I suppose it does have a roof on in case it rains and we could just about fit some chairs in there,' said Amy thinking out loud.

'Oh go on that will be brilliant!' urged Megan. 'Like a flying glamping experience.'

So, after they had emptied out various garden tools and dragged some kitchen chairs inside, the shed was ready to be relaunched as their transport for the evening.

'I feel bad,' said Marley as they sprinkled flying fuel around it and all took their seats. 'I'm the wizard here and I should be able to take you there without the using any flying fuel. It was one of those things I could never manage at the academy. Otherwise, I would have left on a broomstick years ago.'

'Well don't worry. You have all the time you want to practise your spells now without that uncle of yours watching your every move,' said Sabe as he closed the shed door. It was just in time as the shed was beginning to lift away from the ground.

'Take us to the famous Toast restaurant!' they all shouted.

'And happy birthday to me!' added Marley with a huge smile on his face.

What Happened at the Talent Show

As they landed in the restaurant grounds they needn't have been embarrassed about their chosen form of transport. All around were beautifully dressed fairy people in carriages being drawn by crow chauffeurs who were wearing bow ties, elegant witches in pointed fur trimmed hats and fine jewellery and groups of wizards in silver-edged robes being warmly greeted by pixies at the front door. There were people arriving on flying horses, on flying rugs, they even saw what looked like a helicopter fashioned from dried leaves with sycamore seed propellers whirring around as it landed next to them.

'I wish we could have brought our party clothes,' said Megan as she looked wistfully down at her leggings and trainers.

'I could try a spell to make you some,' suggested Marley. 'I managed it once for one of my teachers. She had one glittery red shoe and half a dress, and she was so angry with me because the whole class saw her underwear, but I think I've improved since then.' Megan smiled gratefully at him. 'It's okay Marley, maybe next time.'

They were all welcomed into the restaurant by the pixies and shown to a raised section at the back of the room which had a reserved sign on a table set for four. There was a great view of the stage which was lit up ready for the talent show. As they looked around there was no sign of Ben and there was also no sign of any of the mess they had encountered that morning. Every part of the restaurant looked new and elegant. It was quickly filling up with people and soon every seat was filled and the pixies were turning people away at the door.

The restaurant doors closed and the lights dimmed. There was a buzz of low talking from the crowds as they waited for something wonderful to begin. They began to cheer loudly as Ben strode confidently across the stage towards the micro-phone in the centre. There was a sudden hush.

'Welcome everyone to my unique dining and entertainment experience!' he announced. From the side of the room someone shouted, 'We love you!' towards the stage. Sabe, Amy and Megan began to giggle uncontrollably whilst Marley shot them a look of confusion.

'Tonight, we will be showcasing the best talents from across the land and you, the audience, get to vote for our winner whilst you sample the best menu around!' A big cheer went up from the crowd. 'I will of course be around after the show to sign autographs.' They gave another cheer. 'But without further ado I would like to introduce to you our judges!' The spotlight moved to focus on three seats in front of a table at the side of the stage. There were sat a rather large and cheerful looking wizard, a beautiful elf in a long blue evening gown and a haughty looking witch with long black glossy hair and red lipstick. Seated on her lap, being fussed and stroked was a very contented bright blue cat.

'It's Tip!' whispered Marley in outrage. 'She's stolen Tip!' They watched in surprise as the witch poured champagne from her own glass into a gold saucer on the table and Tip began to enthusiastically drink it.

'She can't do that!' hissed Marley. 'Tip is a cat. She can't drink anything other than water. It will make her sick.'

'She'll be okay, she's a magic cat remember,' said Megan holding out her arm to stop Marley jumping up and causing a scene. Tip looked perfectly fine at the moment, she clearly enjoyed the affection she was getting from the witch.

The children sat through lots of entertaining acts and joined in with the applause and laughter of the crowd. The acts varied from amazing to very silly. There was a gnome who could gargle songs whilst juggling, a group of pixies that could perform acrobatics and make themselves spin so fast they looked like cyclones. Some of the acts had real talent, like the young wizard who played the guitar and sang sad songs with a far-away look upon his face. Everyone loved the dancing witch with her two cats that stood on their hind legs and balanced like ballerinas as they skipped effortlessly from one side of the stage to the other.

The pixie waiters served a selection of small samples of every dish on the menu which was washed down with fizzy drinks that changed colour every time the drinker laughed. Finally, there was an interlude in the show. Megan pushed her plate away from her.

'I never ever want to see a piece of toast again as long as I live,' she said as the tables around them ordered seconds and thirds and spoke loud compliments to the waiters about how they couldn't get enough of the wonderful food. Marley ate slowly, savouring each mouthful with his eyes closed.

'We should invite him to our house for breakfast. He'll think he's gone to heaven,' said Sabe.

The lights went on briefly and the guests and judges began to mingle and queue up at the bar. A group of children who were about their age wearing High Hat academy uniforms stopped in surprise and nudged each other as they walked past their table.

'Look isn't that Marley?' one of them said out loud and pointed at where Marley was sat quietly enjoying his birthday dinner.

'So it is! Hey Marley, you useless fool. Have you managed to complete a spell yet or are you still struggling with the contents page!' the group laughed out loud. Marley stopped eating and froze like an animal caught in car headlights.

'Haven't your parents bought you a new uniform yet?...Oh I forgot, you don't have any!' The group laughed and tears began to form in Marley's eyes. He wanted to say something brave to shut them up but his mind was blank. His body stung from head to toe with shame, so he stared down at his plate in case anyone saw him cry.

'Leave him alone,' shouted Sabe. 'You'll have egg on your face when Marley wins the talent show!'

The group of students chuckled. Marley looked at Sabe in alarm and shook his head to warn him to say no more.

'Marley can't win at anything. He's stupid,' announced another of the academy students cruelly.

'Well, have egg on your face anyway!' called Megan and launched a left-over slice of fried egg on toast at the one who had called Marley stupid. The egg landed with precision on top of his head and the toast slid slowly down and lodged itself behind his pointed ear. Megan looked very pleased, and the group of students began to laugh at their friend. Other diners who were sitting nearby stopped and stared at the commotion in horror.

'They were bullying our friend for entertainment,' Sabe tried to explain as two stocky pixie security staff stamped over and hauled Sabe and Megan out of their seats to show them the door.

'Why don't you throw *them* out!' shouted Megan.

'They started it. We are VIP guests enjoying the show!' Sabe protested loudly all the way to the front door. Amy rushed to the bar to ask for Ben and demand he intervene.

Within minutes Ben was at the entrance demanding to know what was going on whilst the pixies tried to bundle Megan and Sabe out into the car park. Ben motioned at them to stop. The children did their best to hurriedly explain.

'Let them go,' he commanded the pixies. He then whispered to his siblings. 'None of my diners will understand why your behaviour has not got you thrown out. This is a high-class place so you had better think of what excuse I am going to give anyone that asks for letting you stay.'

'That's easy!' said Sabe. 'We are entering the talent show as group of many talents!' Ben considered the offer.

'Yes,' said Amy. 'Megan can dance, Sabe can do a rap and I can sing.'

'Well don't do it too well,' he warned them. 'If you win and then people find out we're related they will say it's a fix. What about your friend Marley? What can he do?'

'Oh, he can do magic,' said Megan. 'But not always, just some of the time.'

'That's fine,' said Ben. 'A foursome variety act. That could work very well. I'll announce you now.' He then walked off towards the stage leaving the children to be escorted back to their seats by the pixies.

When Marley heard he was to perform magic on stage he said he wanted to go home. Being called names was one thing but putting himself on the stage to be the subject of even more ridicule was even more distressing. At once he wished he had put on the outfit Tip had bought him. He was now painfully self-conscious of his school uniform and how it made him stand out as an academy wizard, an identity that he knew was unsuited to him. The audience would expect more from a genuine wizard. He knew a few spells that usually worked but they were beginner ones – hardly a talent. The children came up with a plan.

'Let's pretend your magic controls our behaviour. Just pretend to be casting spells on us to make us sing and dance, you know like hypnosis, and no one will know. Literally all you have to do is wave your arms about like you do and we will do the rest.' Marley looked unsure but the children were confident they could get away with it.

When their act was announced they practically ran to the stage with excitement, pulling a hesitant Marley along by the arm. They had practised their own acts to imaginary audiences in their bedrooms so many times they knew everything off by heart. There were a few sniggers and heckles from the academy children but fortunately they were drowned out by a very welcoming crowd who cheered with anticipation to see what they could do. On the judges table, Tip stepped off the witch's lap and perched on the front of the table. Marley caught her eye and she nodded at him and whispered 'good luck' discreetly before prancing back over to the witch's lap to pretend to be a standard cat again.

Amy, Sabe and Megan stood in a line behind Marley and did their best to pretend to be nervous and shy. Marley began by announcing their act and apologised for his friend's shyness. Megan was doing her best not to laugh as she stared at the floor and wouldn't raise her head when Marley asked her to dance.

'Come on Megan. These people are waiting to see you dance. Can you start moving please?' Still looking at the floor, Megan shook her head in refusal.

'Oh well there is only one thing for it then. A little dancing spell for you Megan.' He looked at Tip who was staring intently at him and Megan. He proceeded to tap Megan on the head.

'*Tippy toes, tippy toes,*
Show me the dancer that wins all the shows,
Star like and stunning,
Graceful and swift,
Show me the dancing we know is your gift'

Megan felt a warm energy rush through her body as she began to dance in the way she loved to do at home. She felt as light as a feather. The crowd cheered loudly. Then as she began to move more a strange thing happened. Hundreds of bright stars began to fly off her feet like tiny lights. They rushed into the air and into the audience where they began to land of the laps of everyone who was watching. The crowd was amazed. Megan carried on and so did the stars. When they started to slow down, she felt it was time to end her act and she stood still. The crowd gave her a huge round of applause and threw the stars back onto the stage like flowers. She gathered a few up and then bowed and returned to the back of the stage to try and work out what had happened.

The delight on Marley's face was evident. He moved onto Sabe and asked him to start his act. Sabe was in character and folded his arms in protest.

He did his best to refuse to perform but Marley was tapping him on the head and chanting.

'Show us something we've never seen before,
Straight from your land that will make us want more,
Something different, to make us shout and clap,
Something your people seem to call a rap.'

Sabe sprang into action feeling more energetic than ever. He grabbed the microphone from the centre of the stage. This time he didn't even need to think of the words to use. They came out of his mouth effortlessly, in time and rhyming. Within the first few seconds he noticed that his index finger seemed to affect anyone he pointed at. As he rapped, he could make people in the audience become part of the story he was telling. A few words about prejudice and suddenly he could make Marley's bullies levitate just by pointing at them. Up they rose out of their seats,protesting loudly until they were suspended kicking and flailing wildly in the air for the entire audience to look at. After a very short while he started to rap about something else and the bullies all fell with a sudden bump back onto their seats as the audience laughed and clapped. When his act ended, he could not quite understand how he had done that and by the look on Marley's face neither could he. Marley glanced proudly over at Tip who sat up very straight and raised a paw.

Finally, it was Amy's turn to do her act. Marley had to pull her forwards to the front of the stage as Amy was doing her best to pretend to hide. Soon Marley was tapping her on the head too.

'Songbird, sing us a tune of your choice,
Let us all marvel at your beautiful voice,
Clearer than crystals, sweeter than honey,
Show us the sound that will win us the money!'

A hush fell upon the room. Amy began to sing. She knew her voice was good as her teachers had told her. However, she had no idea it was this good. The room filled with a sound so pure it was like she was in a recording studio, and everything was being tweaked so that it sounded perfect. She vowed to sing more as soon as she got home. Everyone in the audience had their eyes on her and Amy could see they were deeply moved by her voice but at the same time she couldn't understand it. Halfway through the song there were colours swirling around her that changed softly as she sung. It was truly magical. When she stopped the crowd were all on their feet clapping.

The children linked arms with Marley and bowed in the way they had seen the previous contestants do. They then rushed off the stage, and once behind it with the other contestants, they asked each other what had happened. They were highly excited by what they had experienced and glowing with pride at their acts, but Marley was just looking down at his hands totally puzzled.

'It wasn't me though,' he said.'I know it wasn't me but I just can't explain it. Maybe Ben set it up for us.'

Suddenly it was time to announce the winning act and although they did half expect it, being called onto the stage by the three judges and announced as winners was the best thing ever. Ben presented them with the chest of gold and if he did mind, he did a good job of concealing it.

The glamorous witch announced into the microphone

'Just one more thing before you go. I believe I have something that belongs to you,' she gently handed Tip over to Marley who immediately nuzzled into his cape.

'We should be getting home,' suggested Amy. 'Ben, I think you need to come too, maybe you can brush up on your cooking skills before you come back.' Ben thought about it quickly.

'You're right I suppose. Being a celebrity isn't all it's cracked up to be. I miss just being me and having privacy. Besides I need a well earned break.'

The children, Marley and Tip gathered in the shed they had arrived in and positioned the treasure chest under their legs.

'We can't take it home with us,' said Sabe. 'I can just see people's faces when we try and spend that in the shops.'

'Marley and Tip can make use of it,' said Megan.

Tip stuck her head out of Marley's cloak.

'I can renovate the cottage for us!' she said excitedly. 'I would love a new kitchen.

Maybe a cruise down the Rainbow River and into the old lands. That would be just perfect!'

'How come Tip can talk like a human?' asked Amy.

'Who knows,' said Marley. 'But she's my magic cat and I think she's the best!'

After they had dropped Marley and Tip at the cottage and put the shed back, Marley showed them a short-cut to the rainbow river. There was a tiny boat moored on a small jetty. They got in and told it where they needed to get to, and it began to float off back towards where the orchard was.

'I'm hungry,' said Megan 'Do you think dinner will be ready when we get home? I can't wait to have something that isn't toast,' said Ben.

'Do you think that it was Tip who was doing that magic at the talent show?' asked Amy thoughtfully.

'Well, she is definitely not a normal cat, is she?' said Sabe. 'You never know.'

Sabe and Marley's Day Out

The summer holidays were nearly halfway through when the weather changed suddenly from still warm air and blue skies to grey and windswept downpours that made the old gutters at Orchard House sound like waterfalls as the rain cascaded against the windows.

The children were often called to quickly interrupt their games to find and balance buckets under leaking ceilings whilst their parents did temporary repairs. One day, whilst she was laying towels with him on the floorboards after the latest leak, Amy asked her dad why he and Mel had not just bought somewhere a bit more modern and waterproof.

He had assured her that in a year the house would be completely different and just like a modern house, only bigger. It would be a real family home for them all where they could each have their own room, and besides, very few children could say they lived in a house with so much history and outdoor space to play in.

'Lots of children have lived here over the years you know,' said Amy's dad.

'Very lucky children I hear too, if the stories I've heard are anything to go by,' said Mel.

Amy supposed that was true. None of her friends lived in

houses like Orchard House and she knew none of them had ever stumbled across magical lands whilst playing outside either. She couldn't wait to go back to school and write down some of her adventures as stories. She might even be able to create a book about them one day.

'Dad how old is Orchard House?' she asked.

'Over two hundred years old apparently,' he replied, 'and it was built on the site of a much older house. If you're interested Mel's invited a neighbour over for lunch. He's very elderly and has lived in the area all his life. He might be able to tell you about the people who used to live here.' Amy's eyes widened. She would tell the others. This was an opportunity not to be missed.

'He might be able to tell us about Marley and whether he's really half human!' she breathed excitedly when she found them rummaging through the kitchen cupboards. Sabe jumped down from the worktop, a packet of biscuits in hand.

'Do you think he will know about the orchard?' he asked excitedly. 'Maybe he's been down the secret passageway and visited the magical lands too!'

Ben laughed. 'Yes did you see that old people's home outing yesterday? Shimmering down the tunnel they all were, piling onto boats looking for a tearoom.'

'Shut up Ben!' said Amy. 'Sabe meant when he was a boy. I would love to talk to someone else who's been there. I can't talk to Dad or Mel about it. They wouldn't believe us.'

The conversation was then halted by their parents shouting at Sabe who had absent- mindedly stepped in a tray of paint and walked the contents up the whole of the stairs as he looked for somewhere private to eat the biscuits. The other children gathered in the hall and stared in shock at blue footprints

71

that went all the way up the stairs. Sabe's biscuits had been confiscated and he was howling in protest at the injustice of being told off for what was clearly an accident. After a back and forth argument he walked into his bedroom and slammed the door hard telling everyone to stay away from him and how he hated his life. More towels were sought and yet another clean up job began.

Sabe lay angrily on his bed staring at the ceiling. How he hated that house right then and how he hated his new half siblings, none of whom had bothered to stick up for him and his spoiled trainers. After a while he decided to run away to somewhere where everyone wasn't so against him.

Feeling much calmer and more determined he hurriedly packed a rucksack, changed into a pair of wellies and a waterproof jacket and crept down the stairs. He could hear his mother starting a baking activity with the others and noted with annoyance that he had not been asked to join in. Well, that was fine! He would go and see if he could have a sleepover at Marley's house. It was bound to be more fun than making silly chocolate brownies. He might even be able to find one of those chocolate flight cakes again. He shivered with excitement at the thought and quietly opened the French doors leading off the dining room. He hoped he would have his own adventure, never mind waiting for the weather to change!

Sabe traipsed through the garden, kicking the long wet grass and feeling his feet squelch in the boggy ground whilst the rain pelted down cold and relentless on top of his hood. It was raining so hard he could barely make out the opening in the back garden wall with the old gate that led into to the orchard, but he got there eventually. He pushed the stiff metal gate a little through the muddy ground, just enough to let him slip through, and off he went on his very own adventure!

By lunchtime, in the kitchen, Sabe's mother was just getting the chocolate brownies out of the oven where Megan was first in line to sample them, plate and fork at the ready.

'Our guest should be first,' Mel told her, tactfully indicating old Mr Williams who had joined them for lunch.

Old Mr Williams sat hunched over the kitchen table with a kindly smile, looking keenly round the kitchen over the top of his glasses. He wore a home-knitted thick jumper over a shirt and tie, and the children would have bet that that was the kind of thing he wore every day, regardless of the weather. The same kind of style he had probably had from boyhood. He assured them that he had not been in the house since his father had worked on the farmland that had surrounded the house many years ago, and yet it looked much the same.

'This used to be the farm house years ago,' he told them. 'No farmland left here now. Before the houses, this was all fields and orchards as far as you could see.' He stopped to accept a plate of sandwiches. Megan nudged Amy. The mention of orchards was a good time to ask a question.

'But there is one orchard left. Why haven't they built a house on that?' asked Amy. The children waited in earnest for an interesting conversation to start.

'Well, there's a covenant on that orchard. No one is allowed to build on it.'

'What's a covenant?' asked Ben.

'It's a special rule that was made by the original owners of the house and the one before that. No one is to ever build on the orchard or try to change it in any way,' explained Sabe's mother.

'But why?' the children asked. Mr Williams continued.

'The orchard was very special to the families that always lived here. None of us local children were even allowed to play in that particular one. Mind you, there were a few over the years that defied the rule to try and scrump apples. My grandfather for one. I never got to meet him but I did hear he was a bit of a one back in the day, always up to something.' Mr Williams took some more slow bites of his lunch while the children waited impatiently for him to reveal more.

'He was even found with a girl in there once. That he got into real trouble for. He was older then, of course, but he was supposed to be working at the farm. Pretty little thing she was, not from round here, quite unusual looking. And with all the talk of the First World War starting at that time folks round here thought she was a spy. They wanted to turn her in to the authorities, especially my grandmother, who had her eye on my grandfather for her own. I heard she chased her away good and proper. No one ever saw her again. Good job really, or I wouldn't be here.'

'But did you ever explore the orchard?' asked Ben. 'Or do you know anyone who did? I mean what's so special about it anyway? Its just a bunch of old trees.' He had decided on the direct approach before Mr Williams finished his lunch and went home.

'Me?' said Mr Williams. 'No I've never been there, nor any of my friends. We respected the rules.' He then finished his lunch before anyone else had even started. The children were disappointed.

'Ben go and ask Sabe to come down will you?' asked Sabe's mother. Ben went upstairs. As she was about to give Mr Williams a tour of the house he came back down.

'Sabe's gone and I think he might have taken an overnight

bag with him,' he announced.

Sabe meanwhile was having a wonderful time. That morning he had swung from rope to rope down the secret passageway and onto the platform of the Rainbow River. He was cold and muddy, but he emerged into warmth and colour. One of the rabbit river chauffeurs ushered him onto a boat and soon he was gliding slowly down the river, observing in wonder the swarms of fish in many shades that swam between the boats and enjoying the calm of the firefly lanterns which lit up the river and the platforms they passed.

He passed the Palace platform where he and Amy had seen so much activity on the day of Queen Augustine's coronation. In contrast, today it was quiet, with empty boats moored in a line and the rabbits in their smart green jackets sitting on the bank chatting or reading newspapers.

'It's holiday week,' said the rabbit who must have read Sabe's thoughts. 'Everyone visits the seaside around this time every year. Even the Queen has gone. Will you be going at all Sir?'

'Yes, I should like that,' said Sabe. He liked the sound of visiting the seaside for the day. 'I'm going to see my friend Marley first. I'm sure he would like to come too.' Sabe was starting to feel that this was going to be a fantastic day. The rabbit looked a little puzzled at the sound of Marley's name and asked how he came to know him. Sabe told him all about how he and Amy had rescued Marley from a horrible, lonely life at High Hat's Academy where he was kept a virtual prisoner by his uncle.

'High Hat has always enjoyed being in control,' the rabbit told him. 'Years ago when the old order ruled these lands, he was chief advisor to the palace. He more or less ran the kingdom.

That was before all the trouble of course. In the old days every part of this land was well ordered and everyone got along. High Hat was a popular and well-respected wizard.'

'What happened?' asked Sabe.

'Greed is what happened,' said the rabbit 'Greed was the downfall of this kingdom. There were some that wanted to rule and establish their own order. They experimented with the old magic to make it stronger and more powerful, but they went too far.'

Sabe leaned forward captivated by the rabbit's story

'One day the two rulers disappeared, along with two of their three young daughters. Some say they were kidnapped, some think they were banished forever by those who wielded the new magic. It was a tragedy for Princess Augustine of course, the middle daughter and the only survivor. She was too young to understand what was going on. High Hat arranged for her to be taken to the old lands where she would be cared for and raised to one day return and become queen.

With no ruler and so many using the magic for their own benefit, the kingdom soon fell into chaos. It was split up and now we have some good parts and some not so good parts. High Hat was distraught. Everything he had helped built up had gone. He stepped down and returned to his previous job, teaching. He created the academy to train up the best witches and wizards in the land to one day seize back control. Now Queen Augustine is back, and things are looking up. The kingdom will soon be restored to the way it used to be. This is why you saw the huge celebrations on her coronation day. High Hat always knew what he was doing. He always has a plan.' The rabbit then leaned against his oar, with a dreamy, satisfied look. Sabe thought it was a very nice story with a soon-to-be happy ending but there was still one burning question left unexplained…What on earth was Marley doing at the academy?

Later that morning Sabe and Marley were fishing off the small jetty attached to the cottage garden. Marley was wearing a floral dressing gown borrowed from a friend of Tip's while his shabby academy uniform dried on the line. Sabe was doing his best to catch one fish of every colour. This was because Marley had shown him the unique way that fishing was done in their land. The fish were caught by threading shiny objects onto the fishing lines.

'They are attracted to anything that shines,' Marley told Sabe.

So far they had used a silver teaspoon, some beads from a necklace Tip was making and an old door handle. Blue, red and yellow fish soon came swimming up and were caught when they tried to take a bite of the shiny objects.

'Watch this,' Marley told Sabe and Sabe watched in amusement as Marley put the fish in a bucket and it began to squirm. Instead of struggling to breathe like he expected, after writing about for a couple of minutes, the fish spat out a brightly coloured sweet which Marley scooped up and offered to Sabe.

'Back you go,' he said to the fish and tossed it back where it swum effortlessly back down the river.

Sabe was amazed. He had never been fishing before but now he desperately wanted a go. Marley showed him how to cast his line out with a spoon on the end and wave it gently until they saw a fish catch hold. Sabe reeled his catch in and couldn't wait to see his sweet. He pulled the yellow fish off the end of the line and placed it in the bucket, watching with expectation. The fish thrashed about wildly.

'This one needs a bit of help, looks like he's clogged up,' said

Marley and gave the fish's tummy a gentle squeeze. Out of its mouth flew three packs of bubblegum and then it immediately looked more comfortable.

'Now you can put it back in the river,' said Marley and Sabe placed the grateful looking fish back into the water.

'I love this sort of fishing!' he shouted, proudly surveying his catch. He hoped they could fish all day long. 'Where I come from people put maggots at the end of a hook. The fishes get stuck, then when they die, we tend to eat them.' Marley stopped waving his fishing rod around and looked like he was going to be sick.

'I've never heard anything so gross. The animals are like us, with thoughts and hearts why would anyone eat them? Be like me asking to fry up you for lunch.' Sabe, seeing how hurt Marley looked decided not to volunteer any more information about eating habits at home.

'Where's your mother and father?' asked Sabe. Marley shrugged.

'My father disappeared just before I was born. Uncle High Hat said he clearly didn't want the responsibility of children and I'm better off without someone like that.'

'That's a bit like what happened with my father,' said Sabe. 'What about your mother?'

'I don't remember her,' said Marley, 'so perhaps she disappeared before I was born too. You can't miss what you've never had.' Sabe tried not to laugh at how naive Marley was, then he remembered the fish and how things here worked differently.

'Yes maybe,' he agreed with Marley.

Tip appeared suddenly behind them with part of Marley's uniform in her mouth.

'Fresh off the line,' she said placing a pair or trousers at

Marley's feet. 'Why don't you boys take some of your talent show winnings and go and choose Marley some new clothes. I am fed up of seeing him in these rags.'

'Okay, okay,' said Marley stroking Tip's head whilst looking keenly out at the river, 'We're just going to finish what we're doing.'

'I think you should go now,' instructed Tip and began to gently claw the back of Marley's dressing gown in an effort to take it off. 'My friend needs her dressing gown back.'

'Ok we're going, we're going,' said Marley winding up his fishing rod quickly for fear of ending up with no clothes on.

Ben, Amy and Megan knew exactly where to look for Sabe and after re assuring their parents they would be back with him very soon, they too were heading through the orchard in wellies and raincoats and down the secret passageway. When they got to Marley's cottage Tip was sitting outside in the garden, having bitten open the post and looking visibly shaken.

'What's wrong Tip?' asked Ben. 'Is it Marley and Sabe?'

'No of course not,' she re assured them and asked them to sit down with her.

'The boys have gone to the market to spend some of the talent show winnings.' It's another letter from the academy and now I'm so frightened I don't know what to do.'

She passed the children the letter and her paws were shaking. Ben read it first.

'It's from Wizard High Hat. He is demanding that Marley is returned to the academy immediately or there will be consequences.' He passed the letter to the girls to read and they in turn looked alarmed.

'But why does he need Marley back so desperately? He's

never going to be able to be a proper wizard,' said Amy puzzled.

'And they don't even seem to like each other,' added Megan. 'You won't make him go back will you?'

Tears began to form in Tip's eyes. 'Of course not. He's happy here and so am I. I will never let them take him, or me for that matter...but I'm so afraid of what High Hat will do if we defy him. He's too powerful.'

'Why don't you just bribe him with the gold you have left. Maybe I can throw in a restaurant with it?' suggested Ben.

'That's a good idea but High Hat doesn't care for money.'

'Well we could disguise you both then, say you've moved away. Megan is good at doing make overs. We just need to buy a few supplies. Do they sell hair extensions and make-up at this market the boys are at?' Tip looked oddly at Amy. 'I have no idea what you are talking about, but I very much doubt you can get hold of those things round here. We must try and think of another way.'

Sabe and Marley meanwhile had taken a boat to the market and were busy wandering around the colourful stalls crammed with everything you could think of ever wanting to buy. The first stall that caught their attention was a doughnut stand piled high with delicious chocolate flight cakes. They wasted no time in buying a bagful each and were walking around biting the holes in the centre of the doughnuts and reporting to each other exactly what they could taste.

'Chocolate caramel!' called Sabe. 'Oh now it's more like toffee and I'm getting chocolate chips too.' Gooey caramel slid down his t-shirt and was followed quickly by melted chocolate, strawberry sauce and hundreds and thousands.

'Peppermint for me!' called Marley as he tried to catch

the flavours from the invisible part of the cake in his mouth. The boys threw most of the ring part of the doughnuts into a nearby bin and continued to delve into their bags of food. 'I'm now getting blueberry flavour,' shouted Marley excitedly and offered a bite to Sabe. 'Try this.'

Sabe tried to bite through the hole and purple sauce squirted onto both of them. He did his best to wipe it off his t- shirt whilst the stains on Marley's clothes soon disappeared, leaving him looking as clean as when he arrived, while Sabe looked like he'd been in a food fight.

'See my self-cleaning academy uniform does have some benefits,' Marley told him. Flight cakes finished, they explored the market some more. They found an interesting looking clothing store where the stall holder, a loud and eccentric looking person with a blue velvet coat and purple top hat was making some interesting claims about what was on his rails. Marley said he wanted to have a cloak, but a less boring one than the one he currently wore, so they looked through the selection on offer. The stall keeper practically jumped on them, keen to make a sale.

'See this one,' he said pulling out a thick dark red cloak that shimmered slightly in the sunlight. 'I got this one from a very accomplished and well-known enchanter. I can't name names of course, but you can see the quality. Here feel.'

He seized Marley's hand and got him to hold the cloak. The boys had been hoping to just browse.

'Yes, very nice,' said Marley. 'But it does look too big for me.'

No problem, how about this one?' the stall holder went on, not able to take the hint. He pulled out a small black and white striped cloak. 'Now this was one of a selection I came across on my travels to the old lands last year. The best bargains are to be found there. This one will fit you nicely.'

He began to wrap it around Marley so that he looked like a small humbug or zebra. Sabe tried his best not to laugh as the man commanded Marley to stay still while he brought a mirror so that he could see for himself how 'incredible' he looked.

'Suits you perfectly. For you, Sir, today I can do a special price of five gold pieces.' He stood back and looked satisfied.

Marley unwrapped himself from the stripes and sheepishly put it back on the hanger. 'I just don't think it's me to be honest. I've worn black all my life and it's too much of a change. Do you have anything maybe less bright?'

'Less bright?' asked the stallholder suddenly offended. 'Why would you come to Mr Mahleb's clothing store for a boring dull cloak when you have so many colourful ones to choose from?'

'How about one of these?' asked Sabe who was rummaging through an un-labelled basket of material in the corner.'

'Ah those are the ones I cannot sell,' the man explained. 'They are for the recycling.' He turned his back on Sabe and began to show Marley more of his elaborate cloaks. Sabe pulled out a dark blue one and a dark green cloak with black collars. Both of them had hems that had un-ravelled and one of them had a rip in the arm, but other than that they looked in great condition and could be mended.

'Those boring things are only good for being ground up and make into carpets,' said the man who was now brandishing a chocolate brown cloak in front of Marley and saying it went with his eyes. He was not interested in anything Sabe had to say and didn't even look at him. Sabe turned the cloaks over in his hands to look for a label. One of them was missing and the other was very small but he could just make out the writing in spidery stitching; *'Mr Cherry's Invisibility Cloaks, High Town'.*

Sabe's heart skipped a beat. It seemed too good to be true. He stood up quickly. 'We'll take both of these if that is ok? How much are they?' He indicated to Marley that they should go.

'How much?' asked the baffled storekeeper. 'I told you they are for recycling. I don't sell inferior products. If you like them so much you can do me a favour and take the basket to the flying-carpet maker at the end of this row. He'll be grateful for more threads.' Sensing that there was no point pushing a sale, he spied a giggling group of young witches at the side of the stall and went to see if he could tempt them to buy instead.

Sabe handed one of the cloaks to Marley who immediately took off his old one and put it in the basket.

'It will do for now,' said Marley. 'But I think Tip was hoping I would get something less worn.'

Sabe put his cloak on to cover up his stained clothes. He then hauled the basket up and the boys began to walk down the market aisle towards where the stall-holder had indicated they should go.

'Who needs a new cloak when you have a cloak of invisibility! These are going to be so useful one day,' Sabe told him excitedly.

'Well, you don't look very invisible to me,' said Marley. They were both walking through the market with their cloaks sweeping out behind them. Sabe was rather disappointed that they didn't seem to work but he was still pleased to now own something as important as a genuine cloak of invisibility.

They found many more clothing stalls, but Marley could find nothing that he liked. Having worn one outfit for at least the past one hundred years, it was down to Sabe to persuade him to look at anything that was not black trousers and a black jumper. Marley was clearly getting anxious with so many choices on offer and not a clue as to what sort of thing he actually liked.

'I must go back with some new clothes. It will make Tip happy, and I like it when she's happy. Besides it will stop her trying to choose clothes for me herself. I just want to feel like me, but I don't know what style I want.'

Sabe hoped Marley would decide soon. It was nearly lunchtime, and he was getting bored of clothes shopping. He wanted to look around the other stalls. He had nearly fallen asleep when Marley finally made a very enthusiastic decision. They had been past another secondhand clothing stall when Marley stopped suddenly to admire a three-piece brown twill suit. It was very, very old fashioned and Sabe tried tell him that but Marley was determined to try it on.

Five minutes later a delighted Marley emerged from the changing room in a flat cap which was a little too big, and a matching suit jacket, waistcoat, and short trousers. With his long school socks and black lace-up school boots he looked like he had just stepped out of a history book. Sabe was surprised at his choice but there was no denying the smile on Marley's face. As he looked at himself in the mirror, he grinned so widely that all Sabe could see was a huge cap with a cheeky grin underneath it. It was the first time he had ever seen his friend smile instead of carrying about a worried expression.

'You look nice,' said Sabe. 'But that outfit is from around a hundred years ago.'

'Then it is all the more perfect for me,' said Marley as Sabe remembered Marley's true age. 'I can't explain it, but this just feels like me. I would like to pay for this please. I'll keep it on,' he told the stallholder.

Alter they had placed Marley's old school uniform in the recycling basket, they strolled through the market looking for other interesting things. Free of his drab uniform, Marley seemed more confident. You could tell by the way he walked and especially by the way he came up with the next purchase idea. They were walking past a large display of animals and birds for sale and sitting patiently in lines when Marley grabbed Sabe's arm excitedly.

'Let's buy me a pet!' he exclaimed. 'I always wanted a pet.'

'But you've got Tip' said Sabe. 'She's a cat.'

'She's a familiar,' Marley reminded him. 'The trouble with familiars is that they have magic and minds of their own. They can't be trained or told what to do. They are our equals. I mean a real pet. One I can train to be my loyal companion and take out on walks.'

They walked up and down the long lines of animals who sat on the ground looking half bored. The bigger ones, which were strange breeds of dogs and cats, had tails that were tinged with green or pink and eyes that followed you as if they were about to say something. There were smaller animals on shelves around the stall. They were similar to hamsters and rabbits but one or two of them seemed to have wings sprouting out the back of their fur. Sabe was glad they were not in cages but could not understand why they were not running everywhere and escaping.

'That will be because they have been promised chocolate flight cakes if they behave themselves. The pet store owner will get a load of them to take home for tea.' Sabe found the thought of this highly amusing. It was almost as amusing as the many sets of expectant eyes that followed him and Marley around as they tried to choose one of the animals for a potential pet. When the stall-holder's back was turned one of the animals would whisper 'pick me' and then another would say, 'no don't pick him, his fur looks cheap. Choose me. I can sing lullabies', before silencing quickly and looking demure as soon as the stall-holder walked back in. Marley and Sabe would happily have taken lots of them back to the cottage, but Marley said it had to be just one for now. Then with the same self-assurance he had shown when he found his new clothes, Marley shouted in elation,

'I've found it! I've found my dream pet!'

Nestled on a table at the back were a collection of large grey eggs like small round boulders. Sabe saw that the smallest one must be at least the size of his football at home.

'They must be some huge birds. Are they parrot eggs?'

'No, silly, they are dragon eggs. I have always dreamed of

having a pet dragon. No one will ever bully you if you have a dragon.'

'That's so cool,' said Sabe. 'I would love a dragon of my own, but I don't think my mother would let me.'

'Don't touch those eggs!' warned the stall-holder, bustling over to where Marley was enthusiastically tapping one of the shells and saying, 'hello boy!' to one of the eggs. She was a wise looking old lady with twinkly eyes. She shooed Marley and Sabe away from the table.

'You need a license to keep a dragon and your parent's permission.'

'Oh, I have a license at home somewhere. I don't have parents but my uncle High Hat would definitely let me have one. He says I'm gifted!' said Marley convincingly, although Sabe doubted any of that was true. The old lady chuckled and folded her arms.

'High Hat's nephew! A nice try. I knew your uncle many years ago when we were in training together. I seem to remember him having no brothers or sisters, so he can't be an uncle.' Marley's face fell.

'But I really really want a dragon! Please, I have money. I can pay you whatever one costs.' The old lady unfolded her arms and rested a hand sympathetically on Marley's shoulder.

'I know, I know, but dragons can be demanding pets. They need someone with experience or it's not fair on them or you. Come back in a few years when you're older and I'm sure I can help match you up with one.'

Marley looked at the floor in the way he did when he wanted to cry. He was over one hundred years old. He felt more grown-up than he looked, and was certainly old enough to own a dragon. He would raise it from a baby, and they would be the best of friends. He looked longingly at the table, but the stall-holder was now standing guard in front of it and he couldn't even see past her to admire the eggs.

'Come on Marley, let's look at these cute dogs,' said Sabe and crouched down where the dogs gathered round him wagging their tails and enthusiastically licking his t-shirt. Marley picked up the recycling basket sadly and followed Sabe. All the time glancing over his shoulder at the table with the dragon eggs.

It didn't take long for Sabe to choose a pet dog for himself. A miniature fluffy husky with one blue eye and one yellow eye was soon being paid for and put on a lead for Sabe to take home. He would have to pretend to his mother that the dog was a stray, but she loved animals and had always meant to get round to getting a pet for both of them. Hopefully she wouldn't mind too much.

'I'm going to call him Ivor,' said Sabe and gave Ivor a big hug. Ivor responded by jumping up at Sabe enthusiastically and resting his paws on his shoulders.

'Come on Marley let's go back,' he said. Marley dragged his feet. His early happy mood had given way to deep thought as he continued to carry the recycling basket, looking down and not saying much.

At the flying-carpet stall at the edge of the market the carpet maker was pleased to have such a full basket of old clothes. Sabe noticed to his delight that you could rent a magic carpet for one gold piece and Marley cheered up a bit at the thought of flying back to the cottage on one. Sabe swapped the money for a roll of carpet and as he did he could have sworn the pile of recycling moved slightly. He unrolled their flying carpet and both boys looked again at the pile of clothes that was certainly starting to shudder. The carpet maker plunged both hands into the basket and pulled out a large grey egg which was just starting to crack.

'I think this might be yours,' he said to the boys and handed Marley the dragon egg. Marley didn't make eye contact but shrugged and muttered something about not knowing how it had gotten in there. He then tucked the egg under his arm and sat quietly on the carpet looking straight ahead.

'Come on Sabe, hurry up,' he said without looking at him. Sabe was shocked. He looked back expecting to see the pet stall owner charging angrily through the market after them, or even a police officer. It would be so obvious soon that one of the dragon eggs was missing and that Marley and he were the most likely suspects. The carpet maker was smiling at them as he was clearly none the wiser. Too afraid of the consequences of going back to the pet stall with the egg and seeing how firmly Marley was holding onto it, Sabe lifted up Ivor and told the carpet where to fly. As they began to fly upwards towards the clouds, Sabe held Ivor close to him and said,

'Oh no Marley, what have you done! Why did you do it?' Marley looked down at the egg which was now rocking from side to side and suddenly looked a little scared.

'I don't know,' he replied.

Marley's Dragon

Back at the cottage Tip's worry lifted as she saw the boys land gently on the lawn. Ben, Amy and Megan were excited to see Ivor and loved how he ran over to them. They stroked and fussed him, and Ivor lapped up the attention. When he saw there was a lovely blue cat for him to chase, he immediately ran in Tip's direction barking loudly and expecting her to run for her life. To his confusion Tip stood quite still and gave him a long intense stare. As he got close to her, he suddenly stopped in his tracks, sat on his hind legs and stopped barking. Tip walked over to him and patted him on his head. The children exchanged surprised looks.

'There's a good boy, well done,' she said calmly and carried on walking towards the carpet where Marley was sitting very still holding his dragon egg firmly as if he was worried it would fall apart.

'Marley chose himself some new clothes,' explained Sabe. 'I told him they were a bit old fashioned, but they do kind of suit him don't you think? Oh and when I bought Ivor, he sort of chose himself a pet too. Hope you don't mind.'

The children gathered around Marley who was still sitting on the carpet holding the egg and wasn't sure whether to carry it into the house or stay in the garden with it. As Tip approached him, he looked at her out of the sides of his eyes and waited for her reaction. The children noticed that she looked like she was going to cry again, not at Marley's new pet, but at his appearance.

'Don't you like it?' asked Sabe.

'Like it?' said Tip. 'Oh, I absolutely love it. He looks wonderful.' She then gathered her composure. 'Marley, what is that?' she nodded at the egg.

Marley didn't need to answer. The egg was now trembling with an energy so strong that he was forced to let go of it. Everyone looked in astonishment as the egg shook and the crack in its surface got deeper. Suddenly the crack widened, and two keen bright eyes blinked at the daylight. They were followed by a small brown head like a dinosaur's, four short, clawed feet, a scaled back, a set of webbed bat-like wings and an enormous tail that swished from side to side.

The pieces of shell fell to the floor with a heavy thud and out of it the baby dragon stepped with a boom and it looked from side to side, up down and behind itself at its new environment. It then looked at the children and Tip and proceeded to shuffle over and sniff them. Ivor cowered behind Sabe.

Although he was only a baby the dragon was bigger than him and Tip and came up to the children's knees. Marley smiled a huge enthusiastic smile, jumped off the carpet and said,

'Everyone this is my pet dragon. Isn't it lovely!' He called the dragon over and said, 'You can sleep with me in my room. Come on let's get you something to eat.' The dragon seemed to understand and shuffled on his short legs after Marley into the cottage, his enormous tail leaving a trail of flattened grass and beheaded flowers as he went. The children, Ivor and Tip followed, curious to see what the dragon would do.

'Oh, Marley you are clever,' said Tip. 'You never mentioned to me you had qualified for your dragon license!' Marley felt his face flush.

'Didn't I? I thought you knew.' He felt ashamed then. He was being forced to make up more lies to cover up for what he had done, all because he was desperate to own a dragon and didn't want to wait. Hopefully Tip would stop asking questions soon.

They sat round the kitchen table. All eyes were on Marley and the dragon that was now following him around as he opened up cupboards looking for food. Tip was sitting on the corner of the table, her eyes not leaving the dragon for a moment.

'I have always wondered so much about dragons. I mean what do they eat for example?' Tip enquired. Marley was getting flustered. He didn't even know the slightest thing about caring for a dragon. He wished he had bought a book in the market. Still, he wanted to keep the dragon desperately, so he was going to have to learn fast. He offered it some fruit but the dragon turned his head away and small flames flickered from its nostrils.

'Well this is what you don't feed a dragon,' he said, trying his best to sound convincing. 'They don't like fruit. Come on dragon, I'll show you where you are sleeping, and we can make a shopping list of food you like, can't we.'

The dragon nodded enthusiastically and followed Marley up the stairs, it's large flat feet making the small cottage seem to shake as it stomped up the stairs. The children turned to Sabe.

'Sabe you must come home straight away. Your mother is afraid that you have run away and we had to convince her we knew where you were or she would have called the police!' said Amy.

'And High Hat wants Marley back soon, so we need to think of a way to stop him' added Ben.

'We have to take Sabe home, but we will come back really soon,' said Megan 'Hopefully this evening, even if we have to disguise the pair of you or hide you. We will stop that awful High Hat with his silly orders.' There were loud *booms* from the ceiling above their heads and plaster dust fell like rain onto the tabletop. Everyone looked up.

'Sounds like our dragon is settling in,' said Tip. 'I hope Marley remembers his training. I hear those those dragons can be a challenge at the best of times.'

'I'm sure they will be fine,' said Sabe, trying to sound as convincing as he could. 'Marley is so happy to finally have his own pet and he will be a good guard dragon, especially if High

Hat wants to take Marley away.'

The children left the cottage that day absolutely determined to come back as soon as they could. There was a real mystery to solve. What on earth was the connection between High Hat and Marley and why did he want to keep him in the academy so desperately even though he was clearly never going to make it as a wizard? At least Marley had the dragon to protect him. They just hoped they had a bit of time to come up with a plan.

Sabe's mother was relieved to have Sabe home and was happy he had rescued the unusual stray dog but wouldn't let him keep it until they had him checked over by a vet to see if he was micro-chipped.

'Someone somewhere could be missing that dog,' she told him. 'So it's not finder's keepers until we have checked with the vet and made enquiries in the local area to make sure no one is missing him. Don't get too attached to him yet.' Sabe was happy to agree to this. He knew that if Ivor did have an owner, it wasn't likely to be anyone in his town.

The children spent the evening researching dragons in the local library. They couldn't find any factual information as there was no evidence that dragons were real in their world, but they did find out a few useful tips from legends and stories that they looked up.

'It says here that dragons must never be given sugary food because they are fire breathers and it fuels them too much' said Ben, reading aloud. 'And definitely no fatty food either.'

'I just found out that dragons, despite their fearsome nature, are vegans. They don't eat any animal products and are best off on a diet of fruit, vegetables and leaves,' said Amy reading from another book. 'We must photocopy this for Marley so he knows to encourage his dragon to eat fruit even if he isn't keen at first.'

'I think he should take that dragon back to be honest,' said Sabe. 'He shouldn't benefit from stealing something and we shouldn't really be encouraging him.'

'How though?' said Ben. 'The only way he could return it now and not get into trouble is anonymously. Do they have dragon shelters he could take it to?' The others said they doubted it very much. Marley would just have to keep the dragon but make sure he never stole anything ever again.

The wet weather continued, and it was difficult for the children to persuade their parents to allow them to play in the orchard. The vet had said Ivor needed to be kept indoors until he had his jabs so they couldn't even get out to take him for a walk. Instead, the children had plenty of indoor entertainment organized; swimming, ten pin bowling and visits to the cinema where they had a fantastic time but there was always the hope of getting back to the orchard as quickly as they could in case High Hat carried out his threats to take Marley back to the academy.

They comforted themselves in the knowledge that time moved so differently in Marley's world. They hoped desperately that by the time that they got back, High Hat would still be sending shouty demands in the post and nothing much would have changed.

'He's just a bully by the sound of it,' said Amy. 'If he was going to take Marley back he would have just taken him I reckon, rather than sending threats.'

'I hope you're right,' said Ben. 'That academy was more or less a prison for him. He would never have qualified as wizard or got out.'

It was true. Marley was much happier outside of the academy. For the first time in his life, he was not bound by a set of impossible rules and tasks. With Tip's guidance he was finally having a childhood. He could make up his own games, explore the outdoors until it got dark, and best of all he could play with his very own pet dragon. The dragon, whom he called Cuddles, had settled into life at the cottage with ease. At night he slept on Marley's bed, curling his long warm tail around his body like a comforting hug. By day he followed Marley around like a bouncy shadow, keen to join in with whatever he did. One of Cuddles the dragon's favourite pastimes was eating. Marley always made mealtimes and snack times special. In the first few days he had offered him different things in the hope of discovering what dragons liked to eat. After some very unremarkable fruit and leaf tasting sessions, which Cuddles obliged so not to offend his master's efforts, it was discovered that the food Cuddles loved the most were those lovely cakes with the holes in the middle. Being dragon, he didn't savour them slowly like Marley did, but he would swallow them entirely without even having to bite into it. *Gulp!* Then he could taste a wonderful selection of flavours all at the same time. The deliciousness made him feel warm and fuzzy inside and he showered Marley with hugs and face licks as a reward. Of course, he always had room for more and Marley's still plentiful treasure chest of gold pieces meant that the kitchen cupboards was always full of them. How clever he thought his master was to have discovered just the type of food that he liked.

By the time the sun came back out and the children were allowed to play outside again a long time seemed to have passed, for when they arrived back at the cottage, Cuddles was as tall as the front door and almost as wide. As they stepped off the boat, Marley was sitting on the lawn sharing a cold drink and a chocolate flight cake with Cuddles.

'Your dragon is all grown up!' exclaimed Megan. 'How long have we been away for?' They were surprised to hear that they had only been gone a few days.

Later that afternoon after they had all been fishing and Cuddles had managed to sink the boat, Tip called the children over to express her concern. They were drying themselves off on towels after falling from the boat into the river. Marley was out of earshot doing his best to call Cuddles away from the river where he was happily splashing about and trying to squeeze sweets out of the fish with his clumsy short forearms.

'I don't think that thing is a dragon after all,' she whispered. 'I think he's been crossed with something else. Dragons don't grow that fast.' They looked over to where Cuddles was now standing on his back legs shaking an apple tree whilst Marley laughed and dodged the falling apples.

'Well, he is feeding him a lot of cakes,' said Sabe. 'He's had at least ten for lunch.' Sabe thought back to when they were all sitting at one end of the boat with Marley throwing cakes to Cuddles, who devoured them blissfully whilst his end of the boat dipped lower into the water just before they all fell overboard.

'I don't think the cakes have made that much difference. I think Cuddles is what we call a Gamalite. It's a type of cross breed dragon created as an experiment by immoral breeders and sold on for profit.'

'But he does look like a dragon', said Megan observing Cuddle's brown and purple scales.

'Well, it's true he will have some dragon features and qualities but just look at his tail for a start.'

They looked at Cuddle's tail wagging keenly from side to side. 'That's what Ivor does when he's excited!' observed Sabe.

'That's right. I think Cuddles has been somehow cross bred with a large dog.'

'That's so cool!' said Sabe thinking of Ivor.

But it wasn't cool. It really wasn't a good thing at all. dragons, Tip explained, are solitary, self-sufficient creatures that only breathe fire when threatened. Cuddles, being a gamalite, might look like a dragon, but he was more like a dog. He loyally followed Marley everywhere. He would quickly eat anything offered like it could be his last meal for a while. He had bundles of energy but unusually short limbs which meant that the exercise he needed was impossible for him. However, that wasn't the worst thing. The worst thing, Tip was showing them now, was Cuddle's tendency to breath long flames of fire when he got excited, when he heard a noise or when he was getting impatient. The kitchen table had been reduced to a pile of ashes, there were holes in the doors and the curtains had been scorched.

'Cuddles really needs to be re-homed,' said Tip in exasperation. 'But Marley is so attached to him. I worry that he will never forgive me if I let him go. Besides he must have cost Marley a fortune.'

'Well, you can't live like this,' said Amy picking up one end of the destroyed curtain and feeling it reduce to cinders in her hand.

'Tip, there's something you should know about how we got Cuddles,' said Sabe. Now was the time he was going to have to come clean. So, he told Tip about how Marley had stolen the dragon because he was desperate for one but not allowed to have it.

Tip wasn't too impressed. She couldn't believe Marley could have been foolish enough to think he could care for a dragon without any training or a license. She called Marley over and he came running with Cuddles bounding behind.

'Marley! What do you think you are playing at? Cuddles is stolen goods! You have lied to me. You must return him to the market and apologise to the lady you stole him from,' her eyes narrowed and her voice was raised. 'He should be adopted into a home with someone with the proper knowledge and experience to care for him. How could you have done something so irresponsible! Just because you want something doesn't mean that you should have it. Really Marley! I am so disappointed in you!' Cuddles cocked his head to one side. He knew the conversation was about him but he couldn't understand what Tip had just said. Marley's face was flushed in embarrassment but he shrugged his shoulders and shouted back at Tip.

'Cuddles is staying with me! This is his home now, regardless of how he came to be here. Besides I'm not taking orders from a familiar!' The children didn't know where to look. They had never seen Tip or Marley as cross as this before. They weren't sure where the argument would lead. They didn't have to wait long. Tip's ears flattened against her head and she muttered at Marley.

'A few weeks in the outside world and you think you know everything. Well, sometimes you need someone with experi-ence to stop you getting into serious trouble.' She started to recite a spell in a low voice. The children could hardly make out the words as Marley was shouting and protesting about how he would not be taking Cuddles back. Cuddles, alarmed by his master's raised voice, tried to hide behind their legs, and knocked them over so they landed with a bump on the grass.

Suddenly, Marley found himself glued to the spot he was standing on. Tip finished her mumbled spell and raised her voice again determinedly.

'I don't care if I'm just your familiar. That dragon is too much for either of us to cope with so you either take him back to the pet stall and apologise for stealing him, or you need to find somewhere else for you both to live!' With that she walked determinedly towards the cottage saying, 'Come on Cuddles, let's find you something a bit healthier to eat. Marley you stay there and think about what I said.'

Back in the kitchen Amy was stroking Tip's blue fur in an attempt to calm her down whilst Ben and Megan tried unsuccessfully to get Cuddles to eat some apples. Cuddles turned his back and started to jump up at the cupboards where Marley kept his supplies of Chocolate Flight Cakes. His stumpy legs were not able to get him very far which meant that flames were flickering impatiently out of his nostrils and Ben was dousing them with a damp towel whilst trying to distract him from the cupboards. Sabe had remained outside to try and persuade Marley that it was the right thing to take Cuddles back. Marley was reluctant. He was adamant he could still train Cuddles, but he would need more time.

'Tip says he needs to live with someone with more experience Marley. It's not fair on him to live in a tiny cottage on a diet of cake, no matter how much you love him. He's going to grow much more too.'

Marley was getting frustrated trying to move his feet from the spot. Finally, he began to unlace his boots and worked out that he could simply step out of them and leave them glued to the grass. Ha! He had outsmarted Tip. He would give Cuddles go back but only once he knew he had a good home to go to.

Back inside the kitchen Cuddles was stomping around the table in circles and Tip and the others were doing their best to ignore him. Ignoring a six-foot dragon with a swishing tail is rather difficult, especially when he is knocking things off the worktops; mugs and cutlery were going flying onto the floor. Ben was now chasing him around the table trying to stop the flames, that were becoming fiercer, coming from Cuddles' nostrils. During the commotion there was a heavy knock at the front door which made everyone jump. Cuddles immediately ran towards it enthusiastically.

'I'd better go and save the post,' said Tip. She then started to shout at Cuddles to get away from the door as he was excitedly barging at the postbox and making the door shake on its hinges.

'Down boy!' called Tip, but Cuddles seemed too large to be affected by her magic. She opened the door to two of High Hat's academy goblins standing very serious and very stern, clad in metal armour.

They were as tall as the door but not quite as tall as Cuddles, who barged past Tip and knocked both of the goblins over. The goblins, who had been sent to intimidate Tip into handing Marley back, had been expecting to be confronted by a small blue cat with basic magic skills. When they found themselves floored by an enormous dragon they screamed and rolled about the front lawn with Cuddles on top of them. Their armour clunked and made it difficult for them to get up. Cuddles, who had sensed the danger and slipped into guard dragon duty, was shooting huge flames from his mouth, which judging by the squeals was rapidly heating up armour and the goblins. After much rolling and roaring they finally managed to pick themselves up and shake him off. They began to run away but not before Cuddles had shot some flames at their bottoms. Off they ran holding their burned bottoms and shouting that Marley and Tip were in real trouble now!

Cuddles, suddenly calm now the short burst of excitement was over, walked back inside as if nothing had happened, just as Marley and Sabe who had witnessed the whole spectacle from behind a bush joined the group in the singed kitchen.

'Sorry Tip,' said Marley. 'I'll take him back to the pet stall tomorrow.' He turned to Cuddles 'I'm sorry Cuddles but we need to find you a better home with people who can look after you properly.' He then buried him head into Cuddles' neck and had a little cry. Fortunately, Cuddles didn't really understand.

Later that day the children took Cuddles back to the market. It was as busy and as fascinating as ever. They gave the cake stall a wide berth this time. Marley had felt rather guilty when he had learned how dragons should never be given sugar to eat. That was practically all Cuddles had been fed over the past few days and Marley couldn't help wonder if that had contributed to his extraordinary growth spurt. He had had to duck to get under the door that morning and the slats on Marley's bed had snapped during the night. He just hoped that the pet stall owner would be understanding and accept his apology.

Curiously she was sympathetic, although she absolutely denied that she could have supplied a counterfeit dragon egg. All her dragons were purebred she assured the children and from a good friend who had no reason to resort to shoddy moneymaking schemes such as cross breeding dragons.

'He's a cross breed alright,' she said shaking her head sadly at Cuddles who was being stared at with a mixture of awe and terror by the various animals standing in rows. 'Someone must have taken advantage of your desperation to own a dragon and done you a bad deal. Happens all the time. Not a week goes by without someone turning up here with a sob story asking if I can re-home ones like him, but I tell them there's nothing I can do.'

'But he was from an egg I got from your stall!' said Marley, exasperated after he had attempted to explain many times and the lady was having none of it.

'But none of my eggs would have hatched that quickly! Besides I'm not missing any! I'm sorry. I would love to help you, but I can't.' A crowd of intrigued onlookers had started to gather.

'I don't suppose you get your eggs from your old friend High Hat do you?' asked Sabe. 'As a matter of fact I do,' she said proudly. 'And I'm one of a select few of trusted suppliers. So, you see. Your strange pet is not from me.' The crowd seemed to nod and mutter in agreement with her. Everyone seemed to know of and trust High Hat, so it was pointless putting forward any theories of their own.

'Well what do we do now?' said Megan. 'We can't take him home.' A voice from the crowd piped up,

'Try Old Wizard Manny. He's retired now but he has a soft spot for Gamalites and has quite a few rescue ones so he might be able to help.' It sounded hopeful.

'Where do we find him?' asked Megan

'Oh not round here. He retired and went to live by the sea.'

'Where's that?'

'Holiday Land of course. Everyone knows that.'

'Holiday Land!' said Sabe. 'Of course! I meant to mention that. I thought it would be a lovely place for us to visit. When I was on the river transport, one of the rabbits told me about it. Let's go. We can visit Old Wizard Manny and make a day of it. It was certainly worth a try and Holiday Land sounded like a brilliant day out.

Holiday Land

The boat had been travelling down the Rainbow River for what seemed like ages. The children passed so many platforms along the way as the river curved and swirled around the strange land giving them many fascinating views of their surroundings. It was true that the land seemed very mixed. Some parts were busy with loud voices and crowds of fairy people swarming about between markets, shops and enormous toadstool houses. The houses grew so close together their tops touched and blocked out the light, making the land appear darker. The water was darker here too and the fishes swam around floating pieces of rubbish. Old glass spell bottles bobbed around on the surface and when they looked down, they could see the river floor was covered with rotting broken pieces of broomsticks, pieces of carpet and wooden boxes. Then five minutes later they were passing neat rows of cottages like Marley's, with enormous lollipop trees in the front gardens and paths laid out in what looked like multi-coloured jewels, but after staring at these for a while Megan was certain they were boiled sweets.

She made the rabbits who were working hard steering the boat stop so she could quickly jump onto the bank and prove her point. Off she ran towards one of the cottages that faced the river. She opened the front gate and pulled up a red paving stone like a smooth glass pillow. She ran excitedly back to the boat with it, hotly pursued by the station guard who was blowing a whistle.

'You need to give that back,' said the rabbits who were taken aback by Megan's impulsive excitement. 'That is part of somebody's front path.' The station guard had now reached the bank and was out of breath. In the sweet-lined cottages, window curtains were starting to twitch as people were alerted to the sound of the whistle. Megan, who was by now standing back on the boat proudly holding an enormous boiled sweet started to get embarrassed too. She handed it back to the station guard.

'Thank you miss,' he said. 'Not to worry. It happens all the time.' He went to put the driveway sweet back and Megan was glad to leave. The boat went on, past woodlands and bright open fields. Finally, they seemed to reach the end of the river. It narrowed on both sides and the firefly lanterns stopped. In front of them was a wall of hard jagged white rocks. The boat clunked as it touched the rocks and came to a standstill.

'What do we do now?' asked Sabe. They were all completely puzzled. Would they now be turning round and going back?

One of the rabbits tapped the rock three times with an oar and muttered some strange words under his breath. The sound echoed around the rocks and even the river seemed to silence as they waited for something to happen. Then the central part of the rocks seemed to sparkle and then blur in front of them and appeared to disintegrate before their eyes. Heavy pieces began to fall away and evaporate before they fell into the water. Cuddle's tail began to thump in excitement against the bottom of the boat. Soon a dark tunnel was revealed, stretching through the rocks in front of them. The boat began to edge forwards.

'Hold on tight everyone!' said the rabbits, as they placed their oars down and held onto the sides of the boat. Everyone copied. Marley put a rope around Cuddle's waist and secured it to one of the seats whilst they waited. Holiday Land was nearby but the tunnel they were in now couldn't have looked less holiday-like. It was pitch black and narrow and reminded the children of a ghost train at a fun fair as they continued into the dark. The boat stopped again. What next?

Suddenly they lurched forward and it was as if the tunnel started to open up to reveal a flooding of space and bright sun. The boat began to tip forwards and down a waterfall they all went, holding tightly onto the sides of the boat and shouting in surprise as they whooshed down into a clear blue sea.

Once it hit the water at the bottom the boat was suddenly level again, only rocking gently as the waves lapped on the sides. All around them was calm sea, still blue skies and warm air.

'Wow! Look! I can see a beach,' said Ben. The rabbits began to row slowly towards an expanse of yellow sand surrounded by grass-topped cliffs. On top of the cliffs stood a fairground. The children could see a traditional red and white striped helter-skelter and a merry-go-round with tourists swarming around like brightly-coloured speckles.

'We've got to check this out!' said Sabe as they drew closer to the shore.

The boat moored on the beach. There were a few people sitting on it enjoying the sun but none of them took much notice of the five children and the enormous dragon that had turned up in a boat.

'We can take you home again this evening at the end of our shift,' said one of the rabbits. 'Meet us here as soon as it starts to get dark. Come on Cecil lets go. Don't forget to have a go in the arcades.' He and his colleague began to hop in the direction of some steps carved into the cliffs.

'But where does Manny the wizard live?' called Amy.

'No idea,' said the rabbits. 'Ask around, someone will know,' and off they went.

Cuddles stepped off the boat with a huge splash which soaked the children's clothes. He then began to excitedly chase a crab which was visible just below the tide. He stood on it with his foot and leaned down to retrieve it from the water.

'No Cuddles,' said Marley. 'You're scaring him.'

Marley gently took the crab from Cuddles. It had tiny blue

eyes and opened its mouth. For a moment the children thought it was going to speak but instead it began to cough and splutter.

'There there,' Marley patted it gently on its back. 'You're safe. Don't worry, my dragon is harmless. First time he's ever seen a creature like yourself.' The crab stared up at the children and began to retch.

'I think it's going to be sick,' observed Megan as the crab shuddered.

'No, it won't be sick. It's just doing what it's supposed to when it gets caught.' Marley re-assured her.

The crab suddenly made a heaving sound and spat a stick of pink and white striped rock out into the palm of Marley's hand. Immediately comfortable again the crab was placed down on the sand where it scuttled thankfully away towards the sea. Marley, who had been fishing many times before, chuckled when he saw the open-mouthed reactions of the children.

'We must find more crabs right now!' shouted Megan in dizzy excitement.

'You can have it later you sugar crazy girl,' said Marley, tucking the stick of rock into his pocket. 'We will end up having to take you to see the tooth fairy.'

'But I would love to see the tooth fairy!' said Megan. 'When can we go?' Marley looked at her in horror. 'But why would you want to visit her. She's the land's dentist. Tip keeps threatening to take me for a checkup twice a year. The tooth fairy is awful. She pretends to be nice, but you should see the cabinets in her office. Bursting with decent teeth she's probably extracted from some poor little wizard or witch. There must be thousands of them.

'Have you ever known anyone who's had a tooth removed?' asked Ben.

'No of course not. But the dreadful fairy is clearly ripping them out of people's mouths for fun. What are you all laughing at?'

'She might just collect teeth that have fallen out,' said Amy. Marley looked at her like she was silly.

'Why would someone's teeth just fall out? I never heard of anything so ridiculous;'

'Oh, never mind,' said Amy. It was going to be too difficult to explain to him.

The children couldn't resist paddling in the clear water before heading up the carved stone steps and up the coastal path to the fair. It took them a long time to guide Cuddles up the steps on his short legs.

'He should be able to fly by now really,' explained Marley. 'I even tried putting some flying fuel on his feet but all he did was jump and come back to the ground after a few seconds.'

'Gamalites can't fly,' said Sabe. 'Tip told me. Something to do with their wings being too small for their body weight. She said it's not fair to cross breed dragons and if she knew who was responsible, she would try and stop them.'

'I just hope that Wizard Manny can help him,' said Marley. 'I always wanted a pet dragon. I had no idea about gamalites. Maybe I can get my license and get a real one next time.'

'I don't think you should ever get a dragon again,' said Amy 'Get another cat next time. Tip could have a friend then too.'

They reached the top of the cliffs and what a sight the fairground was. They walked around it and could not believe the rides and stalls around them. There was a 'hook a duck' stall with real ducks holding gold rings in their mouths. They watched as some fairy children caught some and then the ducks, which themselves seemed to be the prizes, proceeded to follow them around the fair. 'They lay lovely eggs apparently. They can sell them to restaurants,' said Marley. Then there were penny arcades where you could try to win prizes. There was a sign at the entrance warning that anyone using magic to win would be banned. Ben had a go at the fruit machine and was slightly annoyed when real pieces of fruit came out when he won.

'What else did you expect?' said Marley laughing at Ben who was holding six bananas, a pineapple, and a basket of strawberries.

Megan wanted to have a go at the coconut shy. She had been good at this before when the fair came to her village at home, so she was feeling confident when she received her hoops from the stall-holder and took aim. Then the strangest thing happened. All the coconuts sprouted tiny legs and began to run away and hide behind the shelves. Megan started shouting in annoyance that it was a con whilst the others were doubled over with laughter at Megan's shocked face and the coconuts with legs.

'The coconuts are shy!' laughed Amy.

'That's right,' said Marley. 'That's why it's called a coconut shy. You have to pay them compliments to get them to come out so you can catch one.'

So, Megan had no choice but to stand there and call to the coconuts, 'Oh you are beautiful. I love your stunning hairy coat. Can I see it?' After a while one of the braver coconuts slowly came out and began to strut towards Megan who quickly threw a hoop over it.

'Got you!' she shouted. 'Who's next? Oh, look at you. Aren't you the perfect oval.' Out came another coconut and started walking towards Megan, who captured it with her hoop. After she had caught three, she was rewarded with five gold pieces, so they all bought ice- creams which they enjoyed with the fruit Ben had won.

'This fair is full of surprises,' said Sabe. 'Do you suppose anyone knows where Wizard Manny lives?'

They asked around but the fair people said they didn't know as they were a travelling fair.

'Oh, look unicorns!' shouted Amy and pointed excitedly at a group of unicorns with silver saddles being led up from the beach by an elf.

'I have always wanted to ride a real unicorn!' She ran over to the elf who stopped in surprise.

'I would like a ride please,' she said politely.

The Elf looked a bit startled but stopped in his tracks.

'I'm not sure,' he said looking around. 'I've been told to take them for some lunch then they will be going back to work.'

Amy's face fell in disappointment and the elf noticed.

'Tell you what. If you're quick you can have a ride now all the way to the stables behind the fair, but only if you're quick. These animals will be looking forward to their lunch.'

Amy was delighted. She tried to offer the elf some gold pieces but he refused. The elf helped her into the unicorn's saddle and she hugged its pure white mane and marvelled at its silver horn and wings. This really was the most perfect day!

'This is a dream come true!' she called to the others and off she flew. The other unicorns following behind. Amy looked down at the fair and waved to the others as she soared over head and towards a beautiful sandy coloured house with a stable block attached to the side. As she began to descend, she saw a lady in a long flowing green dress walk towards the stables with a basket of apples. She looked vaguely familiar to Amy and she was trying to remember where she had seen her before. As she reached the ground, she realised who it was and gasped.

'Queen Augustine!'

The Queen dropped her basket in shock and shouted in disbelief,

'You again!' she looked angry. 'What are you doing riding one of my unicorns? You have a nerve!' Amy was apologetic as she got down and patted the unicorn reassuringly.

'I'm so sorry, I thought they were for people to ride, you know like donkeys?'

'Like what?' said the queen looking puzzled. 'No these are my unicorns that I always take on holiday with me. This here,' she said throwing her arm towards the huge sandstone mansion, 'is my holiday home, and you...are trespassing yet again.'

The elf arrived, jogging up the driveway. 'I'm sorry your highness. She just wanted a ride, and she was so excited I said she could have a quick go. I didn't know you would be waiting.'

'Hmm,' said the queen. 'I should dismiss you at once really.' The elf began to gather up the apples for her and place them back in the basket. The queen continued. 'However, this is just the person I want to see.'

She turned to Amy with a determined look. Amy saw for the first time that the queen really was very young, possibly not much older than herself now she was without her crown and attendants.

'You gave me an enchanted box. Do you remember? The one which you put all the people you had captured inside.'

Amy then remembered how she had given the queen Ben's mobile phone.' She nodded. 'Yes I remember.'

'Well, it's broken,' said the queen. 'The magic screen is just grey. I need you to fix it for me and I need to know how you do this. You see, I've never seen magic like it before and when I did I knew for sure that you must be some powerful enchantress. More powerful than anyone High Hat has trained up. Well, the thing is. I desperately need your help. My family, as you probably know, disappeared a long time ago and no one ever found them. I need to know if they have been captured and put into a box like that one.' She was coming closer to Amy now and she suddenly looked so sad and vulnerable.

'Oh they are not in the box,' said Amy. At least she knew that for definite. 'That was my brother Ben's box actually. He can't do any magic like that.'

The queen's eyebrows raised.'I have heard all about your brother. What a talented family you are. Come for dinner at my palace,' said the queen. 'Come tonight, you and Sir Ben. He can create a very special menu and you and I can talk about your magic. You will help me won't you?'

'I really don't think we can tonight,' said Amy. 'But,'

'No buts!' interrupted the queen. I think you are forgetting that I freed your sister, the one that tried to impersonate me in exchange for that broken box. It would be very easy for me to order her re capture and commit her to my dungeons right now if you don't agree to come. In fact, I can call on my security team right now. She took a glass ball out of her pocket and stared into it. She's at the fair, isn't she? Along with your two brothers and that strange old-fashioned child and...'

She paused and stared harder at the ball.

'Is that a gamalite?'

Amy stared into the glass ball and could see the others quite clearly waiting for her by the helter-skelter. She suddenly panicked.

'Okay, Ben and I will come for dinner this evening, I will try and help you, but I can't promise anything.' The queen's face suddenly softened, and she smiled a wide friendly smile.

'I'm so happy!' she said. 'Thank you. What do I call you?'

'Amy,' said Amy.

'Enchantress Amy,' mused the queen, 'and your brother Sir Ben. We are going to have the most productive evening. Great food from Ben, your superior magical power and I might even find out how to get my family back. I simply cannot wait!'

With that she swept away towards the stables, her unicorns and the elf following her.

'Before you go,' called Amy after them 'Do you have any idea where the old wizard Manny lives? We are taking the gamalite to see him.'

'No idea,' she shouted back over her shoulder. 'They all retire here. He could be anywhere. See you tonight!'

Amy stood alone on the magnificent drive and a feeling of dread swept over her. 'How am I going to get out of this one?' she asked herself.

The Dragon Sanctuary

The others were still asking around the fair if anyone knew where Wizard Manny lived when Amy got back. They had also been told off after Cuddles had relieved himself by cocking his leg up a High Striker game leaving a queue of annoyed elves and gnomes having to wait for it to be cleaned up.

'We need to go soon,' whispered Sabe as soon as Amy came back. 'I think we will have to try to find Wizard Manny another day. No one seems to have heard of him.'

They began to walk back towards the cliff steps down to the beach. Marley took some flying fuel out of his backpack and began to rub it on Cuddle's feet.

'What are you doing?' asked Ben. Marley looked up from where he was busy rubbing the ointment in.

'I'm going to try one last attempt to help him fly down the cliff. It took him ages to get up here.' Ben's eyes widened as an idea came to him.

'We can rub the flying fuel onto something and ask it to take us to Wizard Manny!'

'Ben you are a genius,' said Megan. 'I should have thought of that!' The children looked around for something they could use to fly on when they saw the large leaves that were used for helter-skelter mats.

'I can't believe all this time the answer has been staring us in the face!' said Ben. 'Right who fancies a go on the slide?'

They queued up patiently and when it was their turn, they each took a leaf and began to climb up that spiral staircase towards the top of the helter-skelter.

'Hopefully this way no one will notice,' said Ben. Marley took Cuddles, who was too big to fit inside the slide, over to the cake stand and promised him a chocolate flight cake if he stood behind it and waited for him.

'He won't go anywhere,' he told the others. 'He will do anything for those cakes.'

Finally, when they reached the top of the staircase they sprinkled flying fuel onto the leaves and instead of going down the slides they each rode away. Marley nearly got caught out as he had to head down to the ground first to pick up Cuddles, but when he waved the chocolate flight cake in his direction Cuddles jumped straight onto the leaf, taking up all of the space on it. Marley had to sit on his lap, but they got away in the end. Up they went with the fairground visitors staring after them.

'Take us to Wizard Manny!' they shouted and soon they were flying in a line, through the candy-floss clouds towards the far side of the shore, past the beach where they had arrived -and where their boat was still moored. They whizzed above the cliffs where they spied the two rabbits who had brought them here, having a picnic. The children shouted and waved frantically at them, and the rabbits waved back.

They swooped around the long curve of sand that surrounded Holiday Land and flew for what seemed a long way, past many beaches and small coves until they started to slow down near what looked like a pile of junk on the top of a cliff. As they got closer, they saw it was a house. A very higgledy-piggledy house made out of recycled materials. Surrounding the house was what looked like a dry-stone wall made out of boiled sweets piled on top of one another and looking like it would fall over at any moment. Ben shot Megan a look which said, 'don't even think about it.' There was a gap in the wall which revealed a twisted path made out of more sweets which curved to the left and then to the right and then looped in a circle for no obvious reason as it still led to the front door. The house was styled just like Marley's cottage but made entirely out of junk, so many pieces of once loved things, discarded and then brought back to life and crafted into a home, even if the home was a little wonky and confusing to the eye. It was all very clever. The roof was thatched with old broomstick heads and hairbrushes, the walls were made of polished mismatched stones and pieces of old crockery set into the cement, the windows were stained-glass made out of many pieces of melted down bottles. What caught the children's attention the most though, was the burst of activity in the garden.

On the large lawn a very tall man was dishing out bowls of fruit to group of dragons of various sizes who were seated calmly around the patio on reclaimed deckchairs. Around the perimeter of the garden more of the same creatures snoozed contentedly on hammocks that had been strung up between the trees. The man looked round at the children completely un-surprised as if the arrival of flying groups of people were an everyday occurrence. He turned around and smiled at them. He looked nothing like a wizard. He had long grey and white dreadlocks and his elaborate velvet burgundy gown, once grand, was patched in many places. He beckoned them over and found some spare deckchairs for them to sit on. The children left their mats on the lawn and stood awkwardly, looking at one another and hoping someone would do the introductions.

'Henry, we need some more strawberries and cream!' the tall man called to someone inside the cottage. There was a great deal of clanging and crashing from the kitchen and then out of the back door came an enormous dragon wearing a floral apron and carrying a tray piled high with strawberries. His eyes were cast downwards, and he had the saddest expression the children had ever seen.

'Is he okay?' asked Amy as she took a bowl and helped herself to some strawberries that were offered.

'Yes he will be fine,' the man assured her. 'I found him living alone in a cave in a far off land, said his name was Puff but he hated it, so we let him choose a new name. He's been alone for a long time so he's taking a while to integrate into the group. He's full of the grumps and miseries so we're giving him tasks to do each day to build his self-esteem up again. He took the tray off the dragon. 'Well done, Henry. Now would you like to join us?' The dragon shook his head.

'Well that is a shame because I have a very important job for you. As you can see we have a new dragon come to visit and I thought you would like to show him round.' He turned back to the children, 'What is your dragon's name?'

'His name is Cuddles' said Marley, who was still holding onto his Cuddles, a little unsure 'Ah Cuddles,' said the man. 'Let me guess. You didn't know he was a gamalite when you got him, and now he's too much of a handful for you so you are looking to re home him?'

Marley nodded. 'I don't want to,' he told the man. 'But Tip, she's my familiar and she looks after me, says he's too big for our cottage and he keeps setting things on fire so he should live somewhere more suitable. I feel terrible about it though.'

'Of course you do. It's only natural,' said the man. 'I have many gamalites here.' He re- filled some of the dragons bowls with second helpings of strawberries.

'I'll show you. gamalites, unlike dragons, are very social creatures that need constant company and stimulation, or they can get into real trouble. You are doing the right thing by bringing Cuddles here.'

Cuddles meanwhile was bounding enthusiastically after Henry the dragon, who was walking slowly towards the house.

'I'll show you round after lunch,' said the man. 'You say you have a familiar? So you are magical yourself?' he asked Marley.

Cuddles had by now bounced back out of the house towards them, with Henry at his side, they looked like they had hit it off.

'Well yes and no,' said Marley as he put his arm around Cuddles and proceeded to tell him about his previous life at the academy and how he had summoned Tip, except that she was the wrong colour and wanted to be in charge of him, not the other way round, and of how the children had helped him to escape and even the bit about why he had stolen the dragon egg because he was lonely and wanted a pet.'

The man sat patiently and listened to everything. His face clouded over when High Hat's academy was mentioned but then he laughed at the bit where Tip had turned out to be blue. He assured Marley that just because she was blue it didn't make her inferior in any way.

'The black cat is a stereotype that's all. Familiars can be any colour, in fact they can also be any type of animal. Even dragons. Wizard Manny you know, always had a dragon for a familiar.' The children wondered if they had heard that right.

'But aren't you Wizard Manny?' The man laughed. 'I'm

no wizard but thank you for the compliment. I'm a friend of Manny's. My name is Griff. I run this sanctuary single handedly these days as he can't do everything he used to, but we set up this place together and I will continue his legacy long after he's gone. Would you like to meet him? It's time to get these guys their daily exercise. He'll be out in a minute to help.'

He then clapped his hands.

'Come on you lot who wants a game of fireball?'

The dragons began to look alert and climb down from their various hammocks and deckchairs. Griff began to stroll across the lawn with the dragons seeming to jump and skip enthusi-astically behind him. He ducked through a gap in the hedge to where something like a makeshift basketball court was set out with posts at each end made of old tyres and fishing nets. The 'ball' was made of polished rock. Griff explained that the dragons had set fire to the standard balls, and it had taken a while for him and Manny to find a solution.

'But isn't it a bit heavy for them?' asked Megan.

'Not at all. For us maybe, but a dragon has the strength of ten of us so this is best for them, besides they don't hold it for long. Wait and see.'

The children sat at the sides of the court on the grass and watched as the dragons were each allocated a bandanna with their positions on.

'Oh what a good idea,' said Amy 'Of course, their arms are too short to get jerseys or bibs over their heads. They look good in their bandannas. Look there's a red team and a blue team.'

Across the lawn they saw an elderly gentleman walking slowly towards them with the help of a walking cane, he had a huge bag slung over his shoulder. He looked like the bag was too heavy for him as it made him slightly stooped but he was beaming and waving at everyone.

'Good afternoon!' he called to the children and then to Griff he said 'Visitors, how marvellous! And how wonderful to see you again Frank,' he said to Marley. 'What a beautiful gamalite you have!' He smiled at Cuddles who was still following Henry around. 'And would you two like to join in with the game today?' Cuddles enthusiastically took a bandanna and Henry took one too.

'You'll soon get the hang of it,' he assured them. Griff showed them where to stand. All the dragons were in their positions waiting for Griff to blow a whistle for them to start playing. Wizard Manny asked if the children minded if he sat next to them and they said of course they didn't. He put his large bag gently down next to them, patted it and then sat down. The bag was wide open at the top. The children wondered what was inside it and could have sworn that it moved on its own.

For the next half an hour they exchanged small talk with Wizard Manny whilst they watched the dragons play fireball. It was similar to the basketball they played at school only the dragons played on both the ground and in the air above. The dragons, most of whom seemed to be gamalites like Cuddles, had very short arms and could not throw or catch the balls. Instead, they used their fire-breathing skills to keep the ball suspended in the air as both teams tried to blow the ball towards their respective goals. Once there, Cuddles and Henry did a good job of trying to blow the ball away from the goal.

'How come they don't catch fire?' asked Sabe, slightly concerned over the amount of flames that were zig-zagging in all directions. Griff and Wizard Manny laughed.

'Dragons can't catch fire. The game is completely safe for them. I wouldn't go on the court through.' He looked at Manny. 'Remember that time when you tried to intervene in a squabble and your hair caught fire!' Manny laughed and his bag seemed to simultaneously shudder. Megan practically jumped onto Amy's lap in terror. She hoped it wasn't a snake in there. Sabe couldn't resist a peek and nudged Marley to look inside too.

'It's a baby dragon!' he whispered excitedly. 'Look! Look!' The children peered inside the top of the bag and sure enough there was a tiny dragon fast asleep.

'Is that a gamalite too?' asked Amy. Manny shook his head.

'No, she's one of a kind. She's crossed with something, although sadly we could never work out what. She never grew at all from the day we rescued her from the nursery at High Hat's academy.'

Griff came and sat next to them all and everyone peered into the bag at the sleeping dragon.

'We had to protect Little One here from the other dragons due to her size and the fact she can't breathe fire. She can stand up for herself though. Don't be fooled. She's got her own magic abilities, so she was Manny's familiar for years.'

'She's beautiful,' said Marley, 'and we have something in common. We were both rescued from the academy.'

'When you say she was your familiar, what does that mean?' asked Marley. Wizard Manny smiled.

'Well Frank,' he said to Marley, clearly forgetting Marley's name again. 'I'm retired now. My wizard days are long behind me as you know. In fact, it's time to hand this little one over to a new wizard. Would you like her?'

Marley felt a rush of excitement. She was a dragon, she wasn't a gamalite, she was small enough for the cottage and she couldn't breathe fire. It was almost too good to be true. He looked at the others for reassurance and they were nodding excitedly. 'My name's Marley, not Frank,' he corrected Wizard Manny, feeling slightly confused and offended, 'but I feel guilty about Cuddles. Won't he be upset that I've basically swapped him.' They looked over to where Cuddles was happily playing with the other dragons.

'Oh, he'll be just fine,' Griff assured him. 'He's one of the family now.'

'But I can't do magic. Not much anyway. Won't she get bored if she's used to working with a real wizard?'

'Not at all' said Wizard Manny. 'She needs to get back into practice again herself. It's been many years since either of us did any spells. I don't need to of course, but Little One here shouldn't have to lose her abilities because of me. Besides, I'm sure the other familiar you live with will help out too. I bet you will make a great team Frank, your friend Tip and Little One here.'

'It's Marley,' Marley reminded him again and Griff and Manny exchanged glances. Marley looked down at the sleeping dragon and to where Cuddles and Henry were still playing happily.

'If you really think so Wizard Manny, I would be honored to look after your familiar.' He had a feeling Tip would love her too.

They stayed for tea. In the kitchen the little dragon woke up and blinked her eyes. At first Marley cradled her and smiled proudly down at her but it wasn't long before she was running about with the energy of a kitten and chasing a ball the children were rolling on the floor to her.

'Now you must remember, children. She is a familiar, not a pet. Her understanding is way more advanced. Would you like to try some spells together?' Manny asked Marley, 'how about something easy like a levitation spell?'

'No!' protested Marley remembering how the last levitation spell they tried had led to him being stuck on the ceiling for an hour while his classmates were able to go for lunch. They probably would have left him there all afternoon had High Hat not heard the commotion and finished the spell off to get him down. High Hat had been cross and accused Marley of trying to pull off a prank. He had felt waves of disappointment coming from High Hat as he stormed back off to his office.

'Well how about a disappearing spell then?' encouraged Wizard Manny. You can try it on me? If it's a weak result I don't mind. I can be back before bedtime.' Marley looked petrified. That was another spell they had never got the hang of, embarrassing memories came flooding back.

'Just try Marley,' said Amy 'Remember what happened at the talent show? You can do magic if you just believe you can. You even won an award for it.'

Marley remembered, although he still couldn't explain it. Little One, whose interest had been stirred, flew over and landed at Marley's feet.

'Ok I will try, don't get your hopes up though.' Marley took a deep breath, began to chant and held their arms skywards.

'I call on the power around me today,
To send you on a free holiday,
Just for a while to get out of my sight,

You can come back before it's midnight,

So just for now and without any fear I'm commanding you to disappear!'

In a puff of green smoke Wizard Manny was gone, leaving just his walking cane and over-sized bag on the floor where he had previously stood. Griff applauded and the dragons who had witnessed the spell stamped their feet in excitement. Marley and the children were so astonished they could hardly speak.

'Well done Marley!' said Amy. 'See you can do magic after all!'

'Manny loves it when that spell is done on him. Thank you Marley,' said Griff.

'But where does he go?' asked Marley.

'Anywhere he chooses usually,' said Griff. 'Most importantly he's free from the confines of old age while he's under the spell. I've never been able do it, with me not being a wizard so we are both so grateful. He'll be back later this evening full of tales of his adventure.' Marley was chuffed.

'We should go home now,' Marley said. 'Thank you for looking after Cuddles for me.' He shook hands with Griff and picked up Little One.

'Yes Ben and I have to be somewhere this evening,' said Amy. 'We should be going too.' They turned around and walked to the doorway where Sabe and Megan had been standing watching the spell. There was nothing and no one there except two quickly fading clouds of green smoke.

The Disappearing Spell

Ben, Amy and Marley met the rabbits at the boat on the beach without Sabe and Megan in tow. Griff had tried his best to reassure them that disappearing spells were only ever temporary and both Sabe and Megan would show up before the evening. He suggested they enjoy the rest of the afternoon on the beach. It was Holiday Land after all and wherever Sabe and Megan had got to they were likely to be having a wonderful time. Wizard Manny always did. The problem was Amy and Ben didn't really have the time to wait around. They were supposed to be meeting Queen Augustine and somehow impressing her with magical talents that neither of them actually had.

The rabbits failed to put their minds at ease when they told them that the melting rock they had travelled through sealed up again shortly and that they needed to leave soon.

'You'll be stuck here until next year if you don't hurry up and come now,' said one of them as Amy stared worryingly at the cliffs looking desperately for the outlines of Sabe and Megan.

'And you'll have to live on crab rock and ice creams and trust me you will soon get fed up of that,' said the other.

Ben was agitated too. On top of losing two of his siblings he really did not want to step back into his role as a celebrity restaurateur. It had been stressful enough the first time round and the thought of having to come up with a new menu for the queen just made him want to run back to the comfort of his bedroom and not venture back into the orchard again for a long time. However, this would not bring back Sabe and Megan who could turn up anywhere in this land at any time once the spell wore off. Also, he loved the adventures he had been having each time they visited. It was better than any of his computer games, if only he could work out a way for them all to keep visiting without getting into any sort of trouble.

He stepped into the boat and sat next to Amy who looked like she had the weight of the world on her shoulders. Next to her sat Marley who was cradling the new baby dragon. He gave Ben an apologetic look. 'I'm so sorry,' said Marley. 'I didn't really want to do any spells. They always go wrong but I wanted to show them I was worthy of Little One.' Ben and Amy assured Marley they weren't at fault and it was just bad timing.

'If anyone is to blame it's Queen Augustine with her silly orders,' said Amy. 'Who demands someone visits them with a few hours' notice? It's spoilt and selfish. Maybe we just shouldn't turn up and that will serve her right.'

'But you told me she would put Megan back into the prison if we don't go. Hey rabbits, how powerful is this queen of yours?'

The rabbits shot each other a look.

'She's very powerful. Even deadlier than High Hat. Her family contained the only pure blood wizards in the entire land. That's why they were always so protected. When the family disappeared, Queen Augustine was the only pure blood left. She's the only one that can restore the land back to the way it was before, the only one that can rid it of bad influences. But if she believes you can somehow help her then you must, even if you doubt yourself. You must do as she asks. Why don't we send one of the crow messengers to let her know you've been held up and are going to be late. Hopefully give your brother and sister time to show up?'

Amy had to admit that was a good idea. They might even be able to head home for a bit and maybe time would stand still while they thought things through.

They travelled back through the melting rock before it sealed up and hoped hard that Sabe and Megan would not re appear in Holiday Land. As much as Megan probably wouldn't have minded living off rock and ice cream for a whole year, she wouldn't manage such a long time away from her family, she was too young for that and Sabe would miss his mother and Ivor too much. How Ben claimed to have spent a year away she had no idea, maybe it was because he was that bit older. She had to banish the thought of her siblings being trapped from her mind and agreed that using the crows to get a message to Queen Augustine was worth a try.

They arrived back at Marley's cottage and Tip did her best to reassure them that the disappearing spell was not at all dangerous.

'I bet they turn up here before bedtime. It's a really popular beginners' spell, I've never known anyone have a bad time while they're under it. Right now, Sabe and Megan are probably feasting on chocolate flight cakes and flying about the countryside. Marley and I will be here when they show up.'

'Ben and I thought we could try and get home for a bit and come up with a plan so Queen Augustine doesn't catch us out,' said Amy. 'Time doesn't move here like it does in our world and we need all the time we can get. My head hurts having to think so fast as well as worry about Megan and Sabe.' Tip jumped on Amy's lap and rubbed the side of her head against her to try and reassure her.'

'I'm sorry Tip. I completely forgot you have worries of your own right now. Have you had any more letters from High Hat?'

'No,' said Tip sounding slightly surprised. 'In fact it's all gone strangely quiet, so maybe when Cuddles chased his goblins away it made him think twice about threatening us.'

'That's good,' said Ben 'You should have seen how happy Cuddles was at the sanctuary with all the other gamalites. Actually, Marley has something to show you, don't you Marley?'

Marley's popped up from behind Ben with a cheeky grin so Tip knew they had an announcement.

'Oh Marley whatever have you been up to now? Do I really want to hear this?' She put a paw dramatically over her eyes. Marley stepped towards the kitchen table and unwrapped Little One from the blanket he had carried her all the way home in. Little One flapped her tiny wings and looked around at her new home in wonder. Tip jumped up at the table to investigate and walked slowly around Little One.

'Another dragon Marley?'

'Yes Tip, Wizard Manny said she will never ever grow. She is going to be tiny forever and ever and you will be pleased to know that she can't breathe fire and she's a familiar so she can help us both. If fact she's just like you.'

Tip gently reached out a paw to touch Little One gently on her face.

'Just like me,' she said quietly under her breath. There was an awkward silence as Tip studied Little One closely. The children hoped that Tip wasn't about to object to Marley's new dragon. The silence seemed to go on a little longer than they expected as Tip and Little One sat on the table and looked directly at one another. You could have heard a pin drop in that kitchen.

'What is it Tip? Don't you like her?' asked Marley.

'Like her?' said Tip turning around and sitting straight up. She looked emotional again. 'I think she's adorable but Marley, she's not a dragon.' The children were confused

'But she's not a gamalite!' protested Marley. 'She's a dragon. Look she's got normal length arms and everything. You are being unfair. She is a dragon, she's my dragon and her name is Little One!'

'She's not a dragon and she's not called Little One,' said Tip and began to wash the Little One with her tongue. Everyone watched as the most unbelievable thing started to happen.

The dragon began to fade as if Tip was washing her away and in her place stood a little girl of about four years old with curly

hair tied in a bow, a frilly pinafore and buttoned up boots. She blinked with long eyelashes and looked wide-eyed around the room and at the children. The children who were pinned to the spot not quite believing what they were seeing. When she was fully formed and there was no sign of a dragon left Tip stepped back and said in a shaky voice.

'It's Luna!' she's come back.'

What Happened to Sabe and Megan

Megan and Sabe remembered standing in Wizard Manny and Griffs kitchen watching in awe as Marley did his disappearing spell. For someone who claimed to be able to do very little magic they had to admit that what Marley could do was very impressive. The old wizard had disappeared in a split second in front of their eyes leaving just a haze of green smoke behind. Sabe looked at Megan to see that her reaction was as astonished as his own. He opened his mouth to say something when he noticed that the bottom half of Megan's body had also disappeared, and he was so shocked he could do nothing but point at it to show her. She looked at his arm and tried to scream but no sound came out. His arm which had been there a second ago, had suddenly disappeared leaving a wisp of green smoke.

Sabe looked down to see his shoulder follow, then his torso. He tried to shout and attract the attention of the others who were applauding Marley. His voice had disappeared. He tried to grab Megan with his other arm but clutched air as she disappeared in front of him and could do nothing as his opposite arm also turned to green smoke. Then there was a split second and a flash of green and suddenly they were both back in one piece. He grabbed Megan who was whole again and was relieved to feel his arms contact her and that they were both solid. She looked at him in half panic, half amusement.

'What happened?'

'I think we disappeared too for a few seconds.'

Sabe laughed with relief that he still existed. He looked around. They were no longer in Wizard Manny's kitchen. They were in a wide-open space rather like a village green but the skies were grey and there was not a person nor a building to be seen, only a triangle of grass under their feet and some bare trees around the perimeter. Above them the specks of small creatures with dark webbed wings zig-zagged quickly against the cloudless sky.

'Are they bats?' asked Megan. 'Where are we? I don't think I like this place Sabe.'

Sabe looked up. The creatures were bats and this place felt slightly familiar to him but not in a good way. He started to walk forwards in the hope that he would find a building with some lights on, any where he could ask for help and find his way back to the others, Megan clinging determinedly onto his hand. Before long they could see the outline of a signpost which said, 'High Town' and 'Village Centre' in one direction and 'High Hat's Academy' in the other. Sabe suddenly remembered being there before on the first day they had discovered the land that lay within the orchard, when he and Amy had found themselves on the platform that had led them to the strange village shops and to High Hat's Academy. It had been a dark sort of place then with gloomy skies but it was darker still now, possibly even night time judging by the fact that they could hardly see in front of them.

'We should head for the Academy. We didn't have a great experience first time round, but it was a case of mistaken identity. Perhaps we can get someone there to help us. The shops will all be closed in High Town.'

'But High Hat is a bad person,' said Megan. 'He was awful to Marley and still is. We can't trust him.'

'We won't even see him,' said Sabe. 'Besides Marley reckons he's just a bad-tempered sort of person but harmless, and the rabbits that drive the Rainbow River boats told me he's very clever but he's frustrated at what the kingdom has become since Queen Augustine's family disappeared years ago.'

'Well I don't think we should go,' said Megan determinedly. 'He sounds like a beast. I vote we go to that shopping centre you and Amy found and break in to one of those shops. I bet none of them have any burglar alarms. We could have a midnight feast on those cakes and take all the gold coins we can find. Then in the morning we could hitch a ride back to Marley's cottage.'

Sabe laughed.

'You must have really enjoyed your time in prison Megan, but I'm not sure it's where I want to be ending up. I want to go home with the others and see my mother and Ivor. Maybe we should split and each do what we think best.'

'No!' said Megan, clutching Sabe's hand tighter. 'I was joking, sort of. I'll come to the Academy with you to try and get help.'

They followed the direction of the sign along a path that they couldn't see but which crunched under their feet. They saw no one and heard nothing, not even the wheels of one of the vans that the Academy goblins had picked Sabe and Amy up on their first visit.

After a short while they were relieved to see a high stone wall and the turrets of the Academy come into view. Large iron gates stood open in front of a long drive, and they were relieved to see lights on behind some of the leaded windows. They walked slowly and cautiously up the drive and to the large stone archway that looked like the main entrance. A thick wooden door lay open as if they were expecting visitors and they were glad that they were able to walk straight through.

'We just need to find some teachers', whispered Sabe. 'We can ask them to help us and they should be able to. You can always trust a teacher.'

Megan hoped he was right.

They found themselves in a large bright entrance hall with a flagged stone floor and a huge staircase that swept upwards and then to the left and the right. In front of them was a long table with a couple of stern-faced witches looking at paperwork. The one of them nudged the other and they looked up, their faces breaking into welcoming smiles.

'Ah there you both are!' said one of the witches as she re adjusted her pointed hat and ticked off her paperwork. 'Every year there are always a couple of stragglers. I suppose your parents were too busy to bring you along in person. Never mind you're here now, and we will make sure you settle in in no time!'

'Please Miss,' said Sabe. 'Megan and I are lost, and we need to find our way back to Wizard Manny's house in Holiday Land or the home of our friends Marley and Tip. We're not students here.'

The witches looked at each other vaguely amused. 'Every year there is always one! Or two in this case. Now children, you are here because you have been personally selected. You mustn't be afraid. This is the best school of its kind and you will have a wonderful time here as well as learning to develop your craft.'

She stepped out from behind the table followed by the other witch and looked Sabe and Megan up and down. She sniffed the air and turned to her colleague who was wrinkling her nose.

'Can you smell what I can smell?' The other witch nodded. 'I certainly can Miss Hagworth. That's a disappearing spell if ever I smelled one. They really have been trying their best to avoid the start of term.' Sabe started to panic.

'No! We already go to school. We're not witches or wizards we're just a normal boy and girl with no magic. We are lost and we came here to ask for help!'

It was too late. Miss Hagworth had put an arm round each of their shoulders and was starting to walk with them down a corridor. They wouldn't have gone only they were no longer in control of their feet which seemed to have a mind of their own.

'Now now, come along children. Let's get you changed and fed before we settle you down in your new dormitory for the evening.'

Megan looked at Sabe for guidance and he whispered, 'just go along with it for now while I figure something out.'

Along the corridor they marched briskly with Miss Hagworth's arms around them and the other teacher following closely behind. They soon came to a door which opened into what looked like a storeroom with shelves piled high with black fabric and boxes. Miss Hagworth and her colleague, whom they soon learned was called Miss Whizzity, immediately collected various items from the shelves and presented both Sabe and Megan with piles of folded clothing.

'Trousers, shirts, jumpers, indoor cloaks, outdoor mantles, shoes, hats and the all- important beginners automatic broomsticks and games kits.'

They plonked them purposely down into the children's arms.

'There you go. Get changed and we'll take you to the dining hall to meet the others.'

Sabe suddenly remembered something important.

'We're not witches or wizards and we can prove it, look!' He pointed to both his ears and then moved Megan's hair back to show them hers.

'See! Human ears!'

'Nice try,' laughed Miss Whizzity and immediately tapped them both on the head. Sabe watched in horror as Megan's ears suddenly grew pointed at the top. He felt his own and sure enough they too were pointed. Megan started to laugh at the sight of Sabe's ears.

'Now we will leave you alone to get changed and collect you in five minutes.' with that they both swept out of the room and locked the door behind them.

'What is it about this place and mistaken identities and locking people in rooms?' said Megan. 'I hope these ears go back to normal because there is no way I can go home looking like this!'

'I'm sure they will,' said Sabe. 'Besides didn't you hear Wizard Manny or Griff say that the disappearing spell wears off quickly. We will be back with the others before long. I reckon we should just try and enjoy the experience. Haven't you ever wondered what it would be really like to be a witch or wizard? Well, here's our chance to find out!'

'I think I preferred being a Queen for a day actually,' said Megan but reluctantly agreed to get dressed.

Five minutes later they were told to rest their brooms in the corridor and were being marched into a huge dining room with rows of long heavy wood tables and benches, and coats of arms and shields adorning the walls. The windows dotted along the lengths of the walls were high and leaded and on the ceilings were huge iron chandeliers burning with many candles. Dominating the scene were large volumes of children around their age busy swarming around the room, with plates piled high with delicious looking food collected from a buffet area at the back. The atmosphere was full of chatter and buzzing with excitement. It did look like fun.

Among the students were dining room attendants which to their delight were all dragons in aprons and caps. They waved them along to help themselves to dinner and so they quickly filled up their plates with some interesting looking food and tried to blend into their new surroundings.

They sat close together on a bench observing the bustle of the hall and discussing in low voices how wonderful it would be to learn some real spells and to try and ride their automatic broomsticks. They were just getting used to their temporary adventure when one of the other students started to point at Megan and whisper to his friends. Before long they were being studied intently by a group of boy wizards who were laughing and nudging each other.

'That's definitely her!' remarked one of the boys and they continued to whisper to each other. Megan was suddenly worried and thought she recognized some of them.

'Sabe, I think those are the boys that were picking on Marley at Toast restaurant. I threw an egg over one of them,' she whispered. Sabe looked up. They certainly did look familiar.

A jug that had been on the boy's table began to float up through the air and came to rest over Megan's head. She ducked to one side, but the jug followed her. It began to tip sideways, and pink custard began to pour all over her as the boys laughed hysterically. Sabe remembered his rap when he had made the same group hover in the air before letting them drop onto their seats.

'Great!' he muttered. 'This is all we need!'

The custard tipped all over poor Megan, cascaded down the sides of her hat and dripped all over her hair as she shouted in annoyance. She immediately picked up a jug of water from the table and marched over to them.

'You nasty boys!' she yelled. 'Take that!' and she hurled the water all over the laughing group. They quickly stopped laughing as the cold water drenched them.

'Right that's it you silly little witch!' called out one boy. 'You and your friend are going to be taught a lesson!' He shouted at the buffet table and one of the jam tarts from the pudding section immediately sprouted little legs and began to run towards Sabe. It jumped onto the end of the table where he was sitting and launched itself towards his face, jam side first. Sabe ducked and the tart hit the face of a girl who had been sitting next to him. More desserts began to jump up and ran in a line towards Sabe and Megan who ducked and dodged them as they landed on the heads of other students.

The scene in the dining hall was one of pandemonium as other enraged students stood up and started shouting commands at the food on their plates which began to rise and then spin through the air like cricket balls taking aim at the group of boys who had started it. The students' uniforms got off without much damage, with the food stains quickly disappearing due to their self-washing nature, but several of the students had their faces and hair plastered with food as they screamed and ran through the hall trying to avoid being pelted with flying buffet items.

Megan and Sabe resorted to hiding under a table and covering their heads with their long cloaks, peeping out a little to watch the spectacle unfold. More students were joining in, showing off their magic as they made food fly off the buffet table and hit whoever was unlucky enough to get in the way. Those that had managed to move to the sides of the hall in time stood laughing and cheering at the commotion whilst the dragon dinner attendants who seemed to also have a little magic of their own, attempted to scoop pieces of food off the floor and piece them seamlessly back together like they had never been tampered with, and tried to restock the buffet table. They couldn't seem to work fast enough though and they were slipping and sliding on the floor which was soon covered in various sauces and broken up pies.

'What in the name of King Emmanuel is going on here!' boomed a voice so loud and authoritative that it seemed to bounce off the walls. The entire room was silenced and the students froze and looked towards where the voice was coming from.

A short stocky man walked forcefully through the crowds as students moved quickly to let him through. He was followed by Miss Hagworth and Miss Whizzity who side-stepped the dragon attendants who had had the misfortune to slip on the floor during the mayhem. *Stamp, stamp, stomp!* went the soles of his shoes on the floor. As he strode past the table they were hiding under, Sabe and Megan saw that he wore an impeccably smart suit and tie and a cloak of expensive-looking black velvet and silk. On his head was a matching wizard's hat, quite the tallest hat that the children had ever seen. It must have been half the length of the man himself and gave the impression that he was the tallest person in the room by far. It was an illusion of course, for the man was shorter than the female teachers that now stood either side of him at the far side of the room. Megan and Sabe looked at each other and immediately thought the same thing. This was High Hat! Marley's notorious uncle and the academy head teacher.

'You will all stay here as long as it takes to clear this up!' he boomed and the air in the room was full on tension.

'Where might we find the instigators of this situation?' he asked. 'Anyone care to own up?'

No one said a word. High Hat wrinkled his brow in annoyance.

'Fine then,' he muttered and rolled his eyes. 'I will seek them out myself.' There was a silence as High Hat scanned the dining hall, taking in the student's faces and then shaking his head.

He began to walk towards the table that Sabe and Megan were crouching under. The children felt their hearts beat faster as the saw his legs come closer. High Hat crouched down so that he was level with them.

'Out!' he commanded. His voice didn't hide his temper. Megan scrambled out, wiping a strand of custard covered hair out of her face. Sabe followed sheepishly and as he stood up slowly he realised that he was looking High Hat straight in the eye. Why he was more or less the same height as the man. He suddenly felt less afraid.

'Those are the children we were telling you about! The ones who know where Marley is!' called out Miss Whizzity in surprise and suddenly she was next to High Hat looking Sabe and Megan smugly up and down.

High Hat's expression changed from one of anger to a kind smile. It was easy to miss but Sabe saw it. What was the man hiding? He put his arm around Sabe.

'Friends of our little runaway Marley you say? Then you must both come up to my office for a little chat about how you can help your friend.' He then lowered his voice so only the children could hear him. 'You see it's dangerous for Marley to be out there without me. I will explain, come!' and he guided them out of the hall. They heard protests from the students behind them of 'It's not fair!' and 'But they started it! Why aren't they being punished?' High Hat turned and roared at them all to 'Get cleaning! Or no free time today, and I'll turn you all into mice!' and he sniggered to himself as he left the hall with the children.

In the office Megan was offered a towel to wipe the custard from her face and hair and High Hat's secretary, a nervy, skinny creature that didn't seem to have a voice, bought them lemonade and chocolate flight cakes before scuttling quickly out of the door. Megan went to take a cake, but Sabe took her hand and moved it back onto her lap. He shook his head at her. He didn't trust High Hat. He could smile and bring them all the cakes he liked but he had imprisoned Marley in the academy and stopped him having a normal childhood with birthdays, playtime and holidays. There was no way Sabe was going to be part of any plan to bring Marley back here.

High Hat sat opposite them and cleared his throat.

'Let me start at the beginning and then you will understand. This kingdom was a happy place at one time and the King, Queen and their three daughters were like family to me. Their eldest daughter, well she and I were close when I was a young man. Everyone could see it, everyone knew. She and I... we were the future of this place.'

He stopped and composed himself. 'But then Marley arrived and everything changed. The kingdom was tainted, bad ways began to seep in.' Sabe wasn't convinced. This sob story just wasn't adding up and he wasn't really interested in listening to the failed love stories of grown-ups.

'Look, I think you are mistaken. Marley is just a kid like us. Someone who likes fishing, sweets and going for adventures. He wouldn't be interested in stealing your girlfriend if that's what you think-even if that was the case that's no reason to keep someone locked up for over one hundred years. I think you have been a bit over the top with what you've done, so me and Megan would like to leave now.'

He tried to stand up and found that he appeared to be glued to the chair. Megan didn't seem to notice. She had been contentedly munching on a chocolate flight cake whilst they had been speaking. High Hat smiled at her. 'Are you enjoying the cake young lady?'

'Yes thank you,' said Megan as she took another bite 'Marley was rescued from the academy by Sabe and my sister Amy.'

Sabe looked at her in horror. Why was she volunteering this information?

'Oh really?' said High Hat leaning forward and absorbing this new information. Sabe saw the contented smile on his face, but his eyes were hard and intense.

'Well my sister Amy,' carried on Megan, 'she was the one who worked out that Marley was never going to be a wizard, especially after he summoned his familiar and it was a blue cat and not a black one, so they got him out through the window with the help of some crows and a few broomsticks.'

Sabe clamped his hand over Megan's mouth to try to stop her talking but Megan just couldn't stop. High Hat beamed at this new information.

'Yes, these chocolate flight cakes are the best batch yet. You can hardly taste the truth spell within them, I disguised it with a bit of caramel. Nice aren't they?' He began to laugh.

'A blue cat you say? Tell me more.' Megan threw her cake down onto the floor and tried to keep quiet but she was talking against her will.

'Well yes. Her name's Tip but she's not like a normal cat, I mean she bosses Marley around a lot but she looks out for him too. Oh and she talks you know, with a human voice. We've never heard her miaow.'

Sabe tried to topple Megan from her chair by leaning his chair towards hers and knocking it off balance. He simply had to stop her talking! He heard High Hat ask where Marley and Tip were now, and before Megan could answer she had been pushed out of her chair and onto the floor and Sabe had fallen off his chair too. They both landed on the floor with a clatter and could hear the sound of familiar laughter around them.

Sabe was no longer stuck to his chair. In fact, they were no longer in the gloomy atmosphere of High Hat's office but in the warm cosy brightness of Marley's cottage where Amy and Ben were laughing with relief, and Tip and Marley were with a cute little girl they didn't recognize who was giggling in amusement at the sudden appearance of the two new children, dressed like bedraggled witches and wizards. The disappearing spell had finally worn off and brought them back-just in time.

Luna giggled and pointed at Sabe and Megan. 'Need a bath!' she said, and Tip agreed with her.

'Where have you two been?' said Amy in astonishment. 'Why are you wearing academy uniforms and why are you covered in food?' She reached out to touch Megan's hair and recoiled as it she realized how sticky it was.

'It's a long story,' said Megan. 'Who is the girl?'

They were introduced to Luna who was a very happy child that Tip and Marley were clearly enchanted by and wanted to look after. They all thought it was amazing how the little dragon had changed into a girl. It was like Marley had a new sister. They watched as Luna followed Marley around, her huge brown eyes taking in everything he did as she tried to copy him.

'So what happened to you two?' asked Ben. 'You look like you went to the academy and had a food fight.'

'That's exactly what happened! said Sabe. 'and can you believe we met High Hat! He's obsessed with getting Marley back and we were about to find out why when the spell wore off and we ended up back here!'

'Is Marley really in danger?' interrupted Tip, padding over to them on her soft paws. 'I was hoping that we had scared him off with Cuddles the dragon.'

'I think so,' said Sabe. 'I don't think High Hat is the sort of person that gives up that easily. We need to get Marley away from this cottage at least until we can work out what to do.'

'I know,' suggested Amy. 'Marley could come to the palace with me and Ben. If we are helping Queen Augustine then maybe she can help us too and we can find them somewhere else to stay.'

They all had to admit it was a good idea. But first the children should go home for a while. They seemed to have been away for a long while this time even though they knew that when they got back their parents would still probably be decorating the same room and wearing the same clothes as when they left.

Ivor bounded through the orchard to meet the children as they climbed up the ropes that led from the Rainbow River platform and up to the orchard. As they emerged from the secret passageway. Sabe told Ivor off for leaving the house on his own.

'The grumpy old ladybirds will be telling you off soon!' he laughed. 'Or you could shrink and find you have become a celebrity dog in a different world!'

Ivor cocked his head to one side and looked confused. He was just so happy that the children had come back to play with him. He had thought nothing of running out of the patio door as soon as he sensed they were near.

The children walked into the house. It was early evening, and their parents were sitting at the kitchen table with old Mr Williams looking at some black and white photographs he had brought over to show them. They were pleased to see that the children had been out having fun although they didn't recall seeing the fancy dress outfits that Sabe and Megan were wearing before. Megan was sent upstairs to have a bath, wash her hair and the others were told that it was their turn next. The next day they would certainly be heading back into the orchard, and they were determined to find out why High Hat needed Marley so much and they really wanted to help the spoilt queen out. As impatient as she was, she was only young and had been forced to grow up without her parents and sisters, so it was no surprise really that she was the way she was. The only thing the children were sure of was that High Hat must know something about what happened to the Queen's family and Marley was linked to all of it, but how?

The Mysterious Luna

The next day saw Ben raiding the kitchen bookshelves for cooking ideas. He was determined to produce a menu fit for the palace. He simply would not be shown up as a fraud. Besides how difficult could it be? All the recipes in the books were written out with step-by-step details and photos. He chose a few photos he liked the look of and began to copy the recipes out at the kitchen table. Meanwhile Amy was pacing the bedroom floor upstairs and exchanging ideas with Sabe and Megan and trying to think of how best she would help the queen. After much deliberation and many grand but unworkable plans put forward by the others, she decided it would be best to come clean and just tell Queen Augustine that she would love to help her, but she was just a human girl that had accidentally found her way into the land, not an enchantress and not even a tiny bit magic. As soon as she decided that she was going to tell the truth she felt lighter like a huge weight had lifted from her conscience.

Sabe and Megan decided that they were going to stay with Tip and Luna whilst Marley would go with Ben and Amy to the palace to keep him them of harm's way. Sabe wasn't afraid of High Hat and his silly goblins. If they came to the door again, he would jump on them with his toy sword, and they would have more than burned bottoms to worry about.

They went down to the kitchen to share the plan with Ben and found him sitting at the table staring almost trance like at one of the photograph albums old Mr Williams had left on the table. He had forgotten all about the menu planning as soon as he had started to flick through the pages. He saw how the house had looked when it had been newer, with fields on either side and old sepia groups of people sitting in chairs in the garden, but it was a small, less obvious photo that had caught his attention and made him catch his breath.

As soon as the others came into the kitchen, he beckoned them over excitedly and pointed at the photo. The children gasped when they saw it. Standing in the grounds of Orchard House, in the same place where they had slept in the tepee only a few weeks before was the figure of a child in an old-fashioned three-piece-suit, a flat cap on their head and a instantly recognisable cheeky grin staring out at them. It was Marley.

At the cottage, Marley and Luna settled easily into a new routine. Tip had got Marley to re arrange his room so that there were now twin beds, and half of his room was taken up with pastel shades and soft toys. Marley didn't mind much. It was fun to have a little sister, probably more so than a dragon even if he did call her the dragon sometimes when she threw one of her tantrums and the soft toys came hurtling through the air. Sometimes Marley called her the dragon to her face when she was being annoying. 'I'm not a dragon!' she would say, checking behind her for a tail. 'I'm Luna!' He told her she used to be, but she could remember none of it and just laughed and said 'silly Marley'.

As soon as Marley realised just how much magic Luna seemed to retain from her previous incarnation as a Wizard's familiar he wanted her to teach him. It was easy to learn from her. She was only a little girl and didn't call him stupid if he messed up a spell, everything Marley did fascinated Luna. If he only managed half a spell her eyes would widen in amazement, and she would shout 'Clever Marley'. The only problem was that Luna, being so young, sometimes had no idea how much magic she was capable of, and Marley had to keep a very close eye on her in case she got into trouble.

Tip had been very quiet about how she knew Luna. The children had asked her, but she had told them that she remembered Luna as her friend from a long time ago. Luna however didn't seem to remember Tip despite Tip doing her best to jolt her memory. She brought her treats from the kitchen and told her stories of the land from the old days, but Luna just looked at her blankly and then went back to whatever she had been playing with. After a while Tip stopped trying to ask her to remember. Instead, she busied herself looking after Luna as best as she could and teaching her as much as she could, from how to dress herself to how to draw pictures.

It annoyed Marley slightly that Tip never tried to boss Luna around like she did with him. Luna never got told off for leaving her clothes all over the floor or leaving the taps running, it was always Marley's fault. Tip said this was because she was only young, and no one had ever shown her how to do things. Marley responded by arguing that no one had ever shown him anything either and how when he was at the academy, he had had to practically bring himself up! Tip would then give him one of her long angry stares and he knew the discussion was over. He knew that Tip cared for him but since Luna had arrived with her constant smiles and comical, cheeky ways he seemed to have slipped down a little in her estimations. Luna, it appeared could do no wrong whereas he, Marley, should have known better.

One busy morning when the remnants of spell learning was scattered all over their bedroom floors and on every surface, Tip told them they must both clean up before they would be allowed any lunch. Marley and Luna did make a start, but it wasn't long before they found the invisibility cloaks that Sabe had unearthed in the market. Luna held one up to show Marley with a quizzical expression.

'It's a cloak of invisibility Luna,' said Marley. 'There's two of them, only they don't work.'

Luna looked closely at one and held it to her face like a blanket.

'Why?'

'Don't know, maybe the magic ran out, but we can still play dress up and pretend.'

Luna placed the cloak over her head and started to run round the room. Marley grabbed the other cloak and put it on. He began to give chase to Luna who giggled and hurtled down the stairs nearly colliding with Tip. Tip told Marley off, and Luna ran into the garden crying and then Marley couldn't find her anywhere.

By lunchtime she still couldn't be found, and Marley and Tip resorted to running around the garden and scouring the Rainbow River frantically in case she had wandered off.

'She's definitely around somewhere,' Tip reassured a panic-stricken Marley. 'I can sense her very close, try not to worry.'

Tip began to climb the trees in the garden to get a better view. After a few minutes she was down again. 'Come with me,' she told Marley who was stressing and wringing the cloak in his hands in anguish. He followed Tip closely to a nearby hydrangea bush.

'Look,' she indicated with a paw. Marley looked round and sticking out from under the bush was a small shoe and a sock and part of an ankle.

'She's wrapped herself in that invisibility cloak,' whispered Tip 'Sshh. She must have fallen asleep. Do you think you can carry her inside?'

Marley did his best to try and locate Luna who he could feel but couldn't see. Eventually he worked out how best to carry her back to the cottage without waking her up. It felt very strange to be walking back to the house with his arms outstretched carrying an invisible bundle. They put her down on the sofa and Marley felt for the cloak and gently took it off her. As he did the solid outline of Luna, started to appear. She was gently snoring like she did sometimes at night.

'I'm so glad we found her Tip. I was frightened something awful could have happened to her. I love her much more than any dragon you know.'

'Oh, Luna can look after herself,' said Tip reassuringly, walking off to whatever she was busy doing before. 'It's natural to feel protective over her because she's so small but when I knew her before she was cleverer than most wizards twenty times her age.' Marley felt it was a good time to broach the subject.

'Tip, I've been meaning to ask you for ages. How do you know Luna? Is there some kind of school where you two learned to be familiars?' asked Marley. Tip laughed 'It was just like that in a way. We had a lot of fun, but it was a long time ago. I just wish she could remember sometimes.'

There was a loud knocking at the front door that made them both jump. Luna slept on but they both looked at each other in shock. It was too loud to be the children or any of Tip's friends. Neither of them wanted to move. The banging started again, more intense this time. Marley ran to the window to peep out and quickly shot back when he saw who it was. He turned to Tip and the colour had drained from his face.

'It's High Hat!' he whispered loudly. 'He seems to be on his own.'

Tip's fur was standing on end but she was brave and protective over Marley.

'I'll go and talk to him,' she said, but her voice was shaking.

'No, I'll go,' said Marley. 'I'm the real reason he's here, so I am going to stand up him and tell him I'm never returning to the academy.' He wished the children were there to back him up. He opened the door. High Hat stood there, immaculate in his black suit with his elaborate tall hat. He smiled a wide and welcoming smile at Marley.

'Marley!' announced High Hat. 'My dear child. I heard that you were doing well so I came to see for myself.'

High Hat took a confident step into the kitchen and brushed past Marley. He looked around.

'Nice place you have here,' he remarked as he walked about the kitchen. He laughed when he saw Tip cowering next to the table.

'So, this is your familiar? I do hope she is teaching you well. Still blue I see. Never mind, eh?' He laughed again.

'She's teaching me very well,' said Marley. 'In fact I've learned more magic since I've been here than I ever did at the academy, and I would like to stay.'

'Well of course you should,' said High Hat. 'As your uncle I only ever wanted to see you happy. If you don't want to come back to the academy then you don't have to,' he said as he fiddled with his cravat. 'Anyway I just wanted you to have this.'

He reached under his coat and produced a box which he handed to Marley.

'A late birthday present. You always wanted some pets, so I brought you some.' Marley took the box cautiously and opened the lid. Inside were two small dragon eggs that were just starting to hatch.

'Thankyou,' said Marley. 'Although I'm not sure Tip would

like any more dragons here. We already tried living with two, but it didn't really work. What if they grow too big for the cottage?'

'Oh, these two won't grow,' High Hat reassured him. 'But if you don't like them there's a lady in the market that will take them. She's a good friend of mine and runs the pet stall there. I just wanted you to know that your uncle hasn't forgotten your birthday. Anyway, I must dash. New term and all. We must keep in touch.'

With that he turned to walk out, and Tip and Marley began to feel very relieved. Suddenly Luna put her head up from the sofa where she had been sleeping.

'Hello,' she said. 'Who are you?'

High Hat turned to face Luna and his mouth fell open, his face was white as a sheet. Marley put the box down on the table.

'It's ok Luna. This is my uncle and he just came to bring me a late birthday present.' High Hat was visibly shaken. Luna walked over to the table and peeked inside the box. She laughed.

'See Luna,' they are just dragon eggs.' said Marley.

Luna closed the lid of the box slowly and her brow wrinkled in confusion.

'Silly man!' she said and suddenly High Hat was suspended upside down like a bat from the ceiling.

He wriggled and flapped about in his cloak. His hat fell on the floor and various items spilled from his pockets and bounced onto the kitchen rug. Luna collected them up enthusiastically and handed them to Tip to see.

'Put me down you silly little girl!' shouted High Hat.

Tip was staring at the items and shaking her head.

'Luna!' said Marley. 'It's ok. He doesn't want to play. You need to put him down. He's got things to do.'

Luna looked amused. She looked at Tip and then back at Marley.

'But Luna wants to play with the silly man!' She then proceeded to snap her fingers and High Hat began to spin like a top as Marley and Tip could do nothing but watch. High Hat was spinning faster and faster like a ceiling fan and as he spun, he was getting smaller and smaller, tangled up in his cloak. After a while he was just a blur of black spinning and shrinking while Luna clapped her hands in glee and Marley tried to persuade her to stop it. Finally, when he was a tiny black ball on the ceiling he stopped and dropped down.

159

Luna caught him and offered him to Tip. In her hands High Hat had turned into a tiny black mouse. Tip shook her head in disgust so Luna walked over to the box, opened the lid and held High Hat the mouse up by his tail.

'Here dragons, dinner time!' she called as Marley stared at her in horror at what she had done. Luna peered into the box and said, 'dragons gone!' but dropped High Hat into the box anyway. Marley and Tip rushed over to the box to see two miniature goblins inside, waving a net and looking very angry.

Tip held out the contents of High Hat's pockets and explained that they had contained a growing spell.

'The birthday present was a trap,' she explained to Marley. 'He disguised the goblins and smuggled them in here to capture you and take you back. Luna you are so clever! But what do we do now?' she said, putting the lid on the box and sitting on it. Luna was too busy dancing around the kitchen to take any notice.

It was teatime when the children arrived back at the cottage breathless with excitement and full of plans. They stared at Marley who had taped up the box and was holding it tightly as it thumped and shook from inside. The children couldn't wait to show him the likeness to the child in the photo that was now concealed in Ben's pocket.

'We have something to show you,' announced Megan, who along with Sabe had changed back into academy uniforms, and then stopped when everyone noticed how quiet and serious their three friends were. 'What is it?' she asked.

'It's High Hat,' said Marley very somberly. 'He turned up and tried to trick me with a birthday present, so Luna turned him into a mouse and put him into this box with his goblins.'

'But that's brilliant!' said Ben. 'If he's a mouse. He can't harm you anymore. We should just let him loose in the garden and he can find his way back.'

'Only we can't,' said Tip. 'The magic will wear off soon and then he will be super angry.

Luna said she was only playing a game with him; she can't make it last forever.'

'That is a shame,' said Ben. 'You need to get them back to the academy then, quickly.' The children looked over to where Luna was happily engrossed in a game with her teddies.

'We've already asked her what to do, but she doesn't know. She's only four.'

The box rattled and there was a great deal of shouting coming from the inside.

'Can't you eat him Tip?' asked Sabe. Tip shot him a look of disgust 'Don't be revolting Sabe. Why should I eat a mouse?'

'Sorry I forgot you aren't like a real cat.'

'The post!' shouted Amy enthusiastically. 'You have a postal service here. Like we do at home? Post them back. Do you have a next day delivery service?'

'Next day?' laughed Tip 'What sort of service is that. 'We have air mail. Amy you are a genius! I'll go and call them now.' She walked into the garden and started to shout something at the sky.

A group of robins soon swooped down to the lawn. Tip explained that they had an urgent package that needed to be delivered to the academy and they nodded their heads as the children watched with interest.

Marley brought out the box, secured now with tape and placed it inside a bag. The robins each took hold of a corner of the bag and off they went swooping into the sky. Just like that

High Hat was gone.

'He will be back soon and we're all going to be in big trouble,' said Tip worriedly.

'You are going to have to move house to get away from him,' said Ben, and Tip looked sad.

'But we are all so happy here, and we don't know how to start again in another part of the kingdom,' said Tip.

She was right. They were happy in their cottage and the children felt sorry for them. If only there were something they could do to stop High Hat pursuing Marley.

Sabe was convinced that there was. He had been so close to discovering why High Hat was determined to keep Marley for himself. If only he could find out the truth, then they could surely work out a way to stop him?

'Let me and Megan go back to the academy,' he pleaded 'Marley can do another disappearing spell on us and maybe we can carry on where we left off.'

'Show Marley the photo first,' said Amy. 'See if he remembers anything of his life before the academy.'

Ben pulled the black and white photo out of his pocket and showed Marley while Tip went to supervise Luna who was playing with the spells that had fallen out of High Hat's pockets.

'Wow,' said Marley in amazement 'They do look a bit like me, but the cap is so big it's hard to tell. Besides, Tip says lots of people used to dress like me in the old lands and the market is full of secondhand clothes like these so maybe it's just a coincidence.' Ben looked down at the photo again. Marley had a point. He'd seen lots of old photos with people dressed in similar clothing so maybe he had jumped to conclusions. He had been hoping he was on the brink of solving the mystery of Marley's identity.'

'What if High Hat is actually your real father?' suggested Megan.

'Please don't ever suggest that,' said Marley pretending to vomit. 'If he was my dad, I'd be so short I would have to stand on Tip's shoulders all the time, and he would have nothing to gain by keeping me hidden away would he? I can't remember any of my life before the academy. I so wish I could.'

'That's why we should go back,' said Sabe. 'We might be able to find out and solve this mystery for you.'

Marley agreed to try the disappearing spell once more on Sabe and Megan. In the meantime Amy would go with Ben to the palace for their appointment with Queen Augustine and they would take Marley with them. The palace, they all agreed, was the last place High Hat would look for him and Luna and Tip would go too, hidden under an invisibility cloak.

'We are going to deal with that bully High Hat for you before the summer ends and we have to go back to school,' Sabe reassured him.

The children knew that this might be their last visit all together to the kingdom before they had to return to their own schools, so the plan had to work!

Megan and Sabe stood in front of Marley as he recited the words of the invisibility spell once more. In a puff of green smoke, they were soon gone and Marley was delighted.

'I'll be a real wizard one day just you watch me!' he cried as the others exchanged doubtful looks.

Secrets are Revealed

Sabe and Megan were back in High Hat's office where they picked themselves up off the floor and dusted themselves down. High Hat was nowhere to be seen. The remains of the chocolate flight cakes were still on the plate on his desk looking as fresh as when Megan had taken her last bite.

'Let's try and find some student folders,' suggested Megan. 'They might have some background info on Marley, or even his parents' names.'

'That's a great idea!' suggested Sabe. They locked the door and began opening the cupboards. Old dusty files were piled up everywhere and unfortunately none of them appeared to be in any order. Sabe opened up a few with student names on to find paperwork from previous schools. After a while although he could find nothing on Marley, he started to notice a pattern.

'Look at this!' he called to Megan. 'All these students have been expelled from their previous schools.' He showed Megan a few examples.

'Dimity Surespell...expelled after turning the hairs on the teacher's legs into spiders.' He chucked at that one. 'Master Jett McGinty, expelled from Broadway Academy for Gifted Children, dismissed from an apprenticeship with Mr Quick Quack's Emporium of Solutions for selling fake spells for profit.'

'Look at her,' said Megan, pointing to a file photo of an annoyed looking girl.

'Ivy Belladonna Silver, Not expelled from any schools but parents are travelling witches and she repeatedly refuses to conform to their way of life. I thought all the witches and wizards at the academy were chosen for their talent? This lot look like they just liked rebelling,' said Megan.

They looked though many more student folders and found more of the same.

'High Hat has selected his students based on their potential to rebel,' said Sabe. 'The rabbits told me that the kingdom fell into ruin when some people tried to abuse the magic code to get more for themselves. High Hat is a bad person you know. He's deliberately making these children into the worst possible people they can be.'

'And if they have magical abilities, which all of them seem to have, then they have the ability to cause a lot of trouble.'

There was a rattling of the doorknob and Sabe and Megan hurriedly packed the folders back where they found them. They composed themselves and opened the door calmly. In the doorway stood High Hat's mute assistant with the post, including the large box which contained High Hat and the goblins. The box was mysteriously quiet.

'High Hat went on an errand,' Megan explained. 'I'm sure he will be back in a minute.'

The odd-looking creature looked around nervously and placed the post on the desk.

'Can you talk?' Sabe asked him. The creature shook his head.

'What are you anyway?' asked Sabe, observing the spiky tail sticking out the back of High Hat's secretary's suit, his huge bulging eyes and small furry ears poking out of the top of his hair. The creature took a piece of paper and a pencil from the desk and started to draw.

'Oh you're half dragon, then you must be a gamalite.'

The creature shook his head and then drew pictures of a cat, a dragon, a dog and a fish.'

'What, you are all those things? How is that even possible? Where did you come from?'

The creature patted the floor and pointed downwards. He was such a nervous-looking thing that the children felt sorry for him.

'You came from in the ground?' guessed Sabe. 'Only this is the ground floor.'

The creature shook his head and pointed at the floor insistently again. He then rocked his arms to imitate rocking a baby.

'We don't understand,' said Megan 'You were a baby that grew from the ground?'

The sudden sound of clunking amour from the far end of the corridor outside made them all jump and the creature scuttled quickly away. The children looked at each other in horror. What if it was High Hat returning with his goblins? The footsteps got nearer. Megan nudged the corner of the box open.

'Oh no, it's empty!' she whispered loudly.

'Quick try the window!' said Sabe, and they ran to open the window.

'Thank goodness we're on the ground floor!' he said as they climbed onto the ledge and jumped down.

'Where should we go now?' asked Megan. They were in a high-walled courtyard which was empty for now, but it wouldn't be long before High Hat found them.

'Let's go down here,' suggested Sabe. 'I don't think we are

getting over that wall.'

He pointed to some stone steps leading downwards where they could hear the whirr of machinery. As they descended the steps, they could feel warm air and smelled the fresh scent of clean clothes. They quietly opened the door at the bottom of the stairs to find themselves in a long room full of shelves with neatly folded uniforms on one side and huge bags of washing on the other.

'This must be the school laundry,' said Megan. 'I wonder where this leads to?'

They walked to the end of the room where another door opened to a very busy scene. Small dragons in white aprons and caps were hard at work, washing, ironing and spraying clothes. No one seemed to look up, and the children observed the workings of the room with fascination. There were no washing machines like they had at home. Instead, the dirty uniforms and bed sheets were carried into the room and tipped into a long vat of soapy fast- moving water which ran along one length of the room. A few of the smaller dragons were wading in the water bashing their long tails repeatedly into it as the washing was churned and flung about rapidly by their tails and feet moving and swirling about. At the sides of the vat more dragons stood in lines fishing the clothing out of the water and giving them an additional scrub before throwing them back in. Finally, the clothing reached the end of the vat where they were picked out, wrung and taken in barrows to the other side of the room where bigger dragons were pegging them onto moving clothes lines and breathing onto them from a distance.

'Look at how they are drying those clothes,' laughed Megan.

The washing was drying fast. Occasionally one of the items would get singed and a matronly dragon would tut, whip it off the line and carry it through an adjoining door.

'That looks like the only way out,' said Sabe. 'We are going to have to crouch down and creep through the room to get through that door.'

'Don't be ridiculous Sabe!' said Megan. 'We stand out too much. They will catch us, and I don't fancy being barbecued today. Let's disguise ourselves as washing and try and get out that way. What is it?' Megan looked at Sabe who looked deep in thought.

'Marley told me the academy uniforms are all self-washing,' said Sabe. 'They definitely were. I saw it with my own eyes when Marley and I went to the market and got loads of chocolate flight cakes down our clothes. The stains on Marley's uniform disappeared immediately so why are they washing all these uniforms? It doesn't make sense.'

The mystery surrounding Marley was deepening and Sabe really wanted to get to the bottom of it.

They both covered themselves in bed sheets and picked up a laundry bag each which they hid behind as they moved slowly through the room, carefully staying at the sides and hoping that they blended in. None of the dragons seemed to look up. They were fortunately very engrossed in their work.

'I wish I could take a couple of these guys home with me,' whispered Sabe. 'They would save our parents a lot of washing and cleaning time.'

'I think it's wrong somehow,' whispered Megan as they got to the door at the other side of the room. 'Remember how happy the gamalites at Manny and Griff's sanctuary were? This lot are just servants, none of them look happy. I bet High Hat never lets them play fireball or lie about in hammocks on their days off drinking lemonade.'

Sabe had to agree with her. The gamalite staff he had seen so far were low level staff and they all had that same sad look in their eyes.'

In the next room as they set down their washing piles and sat behind them, they saw more gamalites sitting on a bench repairing damaged garments. There were also several more of them busy ironing, spraying the clothes with a fresh scent and folding them neatly. They also saw, to their relief, that they were very close to another door that seemed to lead out of the laundry and into another corridor.

'I absolutely stink,' said Sabe as he swiped a bottle of the fabric spray from a shelf on the way out. 'I reckon those were the dirty uniforms that were involved in the food fight, they smelled awful.'

'Lets follow this corridor and see where it leads,' suggested Megan.

They were standing in a brightly-lit corridor and it felt less restrictive than the atmosphere of the academy laundry.

'So why do you reckon Marley had the only self-cleaning uniform?' she asked as Sabe sprayed himself liberally with the laundry scent muttering about how awful the lingering smell was. He looked at Megan blankly.

'Sorry. What are you talking about?' said Sabe, looking around with a half scared look on his face.

'I was just asking why you thought Marley had the only self-washing...' She stopped when she saw Sabe's bewildered look. 'Sabe are you ok?' He looked at her, confusion on his face.

'Who are you?' he asked, panicking slightly. 'Where am I? Who is Sabe?'

Megan looked closely at him. Sabe's memory had somehow disappeared. She picked up the spray bottle that he had discarded on the floor. There was no label on it, but she tucked it into her pocket.

'You shouldn't spray yourself with something if you don't know what it is!' she told him crossly. Sabe just looked baffled.

'What am I supposed to do now?' Megan asked herself.

The others had arrived at the palace gates. Ben was feeling confident. He had read the recipes he had brought from home many times and studied the accompanying photos, and he was sure he could pull off a feast fit for a queen.

Amy was more nervous. She just hoped that the queen would appreciate her being honest about having no magic. After all, she had never pretended to be anything but a human girl. It was Queen Augustine that had made assumptions. Beneath the queen's spoiled exterior Amy was sure that she was just a lonely girl, acting out a role that had been forced upon her. Perhaps they could be friends and Amy could help her in some other way.

Marley stood awkwardly fiddling with his cap. Luna held onto his hand tightly, hidden from view in her invisibility cloak with Tip under her arm.

'The palace, the palace!' she shouted in excitement and jumped up and down.

'Now Luna, remember you have to keep very quiet as you and Tip are not supposed to be here. If you keep quiet, I will find you lots of treats in the palace. Would you like that?'

Luna tugged his hand enthusiastically and jumped up and down again. Tip told her to stop as Luna's jumping was starting to give her motion sickness. Marley wished that he could have worn the other invisibility cloak but despite trying it on many times he was as visible as he had ever been, and Luna seemed clueless as to how she had managed to make hers work.

The gates automatically opened, and they walked towards the vast white palace with its shimmering roofs.

'I wish I could live here,' said Tip wistfully.

'I think it would be rather lonely,' said Amy. 'Besides, your cottage is lovely. We're going to see to it that you can all live there happily ever after.'

'Well, I would much rather live here,' sighed Tip but no one said anything else. They were too busy staring in awe at the way that the leaves around the front door and windows were starting to turn a brilliant shade of green and bright flowers were appearing and blooming in front of their eyes.

'That's clever,' said Marley as the door swung open to reveal a wide red carpet unrolling itself for them to walk along.

Queen Augustine appeared at the top of a gold balcony that swept around the grand entrance hall and led to a large red carpeted staircase leading downwards. Around the hall were great marble arches leading to many corridors and doors lead-ing off and the children were aware of many small eyes peeping curiously at them through gaps in the doors. Queen Augustine snapped her fingers and looked in annoyance towards the doors and the observers, startled in the knowledge that they had been caught peeping, shot backwards and the doors clicked shut.

'I apologise on behalf of my attendants,' said Queen Augus-tine. 'It's not every day we have the honour of being visited by such a great enchantress as yourself, so everyone is curious. I had to banish them to the kitchens so that we can talk in private.'

She walked slowly down the great staircase towards them, lifting her sparkling blue gown above her delicate gold heels.

'Ooh pretty dress. I want one like that,' Luna exclaimed and Marley had to nudge the air next to him to try and find her and remind her to keep quiet.

'Marley will buy you one if you will just please keep quiet!' he whispered.

'I see you have brought your servant with you' said Queen Augustine looking an annoyed Marley up and down.

'Well, he's more of a friend,' explained Ben as he heard Marley sigh crossly.

'I would like us to have dinner in private,' said the queen. 'You servant,run along and meet the other staff down in the kitchen. I'm sure you can help peel the vegetables and make yourself useful.'

She waved her hand to dismiss Marley. He looked at Ben and

Amy and hoped they would say something in his defence and let him stay for some of Ben's wonderful meal creations. When neither of them met his gaze, he stomped off in the direction of one of the corridors with Luna and Tip following him having a good look at their elaborate surroundings on the way.

Now there was just Ben and Amy left. Queen Augustine shook Ben's hand and welcomed him to her home. She said she was so looking forward to sampling his menu and Ben assured her that he had something very special planned. The queen clapped her hands in delight.

'This is going to be the best evening ever!' she said with the excitement of a child about to go to a party. 'But first can I get you a drink? Beer? Wine?'

'I'll have a beer please,' said Ben. 'A pint if you've got one.'

Amy shot him a look of annoyance.

'My brother is of course joking, neither of us drink because we are too young.' Ben's face fell. 'Do you have anything non-alcoholic?' she asked and the queen suggested they have a look in the dining room.

'I bet you can't wait to get started,' said the queen to Ben. 'Off you go, the kitchen is over there. The servants are waiting for your instructions.' She waved her hand to dismiss a very disappointed-looking Ben. He stood open mouthed in the grand hall as he watched the queen and Amy drift off into the dining room to wait for the grand feast he had promised them. He felt the pieces of crumpled paper in his pocket that he had ripped out of the recipe books from home and began to panic.

'No, I won't panic. I've got this. I'm the greatest chef the land has ever seen remember?' he told himself and turned and walked towards the kitchens.

Marley didn't want to go to the kitchen. 'A servant!' he said crossly to Luna and Tip. 'I'm hardly dressed like a servant, am I? Let's go and explore shall we?'

Luna and Tip agreed that none of them would be any use in the kitchen so off they went down the long marble corridor. As they walked the plants that lined the corridors on marble plinths seemed to stand to attention and even seemed to be growing as they passed by. Tip remarked that it looked like they were coming back to life. It was true, thought Marley as they walked past more of them. One minute they were listless and asleep, and now they were becoming brighter and somehow more alive.

'It's really posh here isn't it? I feel like we are all under-dressed for the occasion,' remarked Marley. Luna giggled.

'Marley silly! No one can see me, and Tip can't wear clothes!' she laughed loudly and the noise made the doors in the corridor open slightly as the palace attendants tried to peep at what was going on.

'Let's go outside!' suggested Marley, relieved to see a door to the garden propped open.

They stepped out into a perfectly manicured garden framed by a brilliant sunset. The rich green lawns stretched as far as they could see and around them were sand-coloured paths lined with full fruit trees and bright flowering bushes. There were gardeners about too. Marley thought they looked rather like the gnome statues he had seen in the market. They all had long beards and long floppy hats as they gathered in groups, stopping with their wheelbarrows and hedge clippers as they discussed the wonder that was the palace garden. They were so engrossed in commenting on the shrubs and flowers that none of them seemed to notice Marley as he walked casually along the paths appearing to talk to himself.

'It's lovely here, isn't it?' Marley remarked to an invisible Tip and Luna. 'I think this is a nice way to spend an evening. I wonder how all the others are getting on? Do you think they will find out who I really am?'

'I hope so,' said Tip, but she sounded sad.

'I won't leave you whatever happens,' he assured her, and he meant it. Whatever Sabe and Megan found at the academy would solve a lifelong mystery for sure but at the same time he didn't want anything to change. He was happier with Tip and Luna than he had ever been and he belonged with them. He was sure his real family wouldn't want him back anyway. No one had ever come forward to claim him. Perhaps High Hat had been trying to protect him all this time. Maybe he should put a stop to the search after all.

'I've decided,' he began. 'After Amy has finished her meeting with Queen Augustine I think we should go and get Sabe and Megan from the academy and just make a new start somewhere. We can get another cottage and change our names, maybe head to the old lands or Holiday Land. I can earn some money for us as an odd job wizard, I'm getting better all the time.' As he heard himself speak it sounded like a good plan. He could feel Luna pulling him towards what looked like a maze and as they got closer, he was delighted to see that it really was. A maze with high hedges.

'Let's play hide and seek,' said Luna and threw off her invisibility cloak. She carefully placed Tip down and began to run.

'Come on Marley, Tip you count and try and find us!'

Happy to be finally out of sight of the gardeners and any other peeping palace staff, Tip agreed began to count as Marley and

Luna ran off through the maze.

Back at the academy Megan was guiding a bewildered Sabe through the corridors and trying her best to explain to him who he was, who she was and why they were there. It was a useless exercise. Sabe couldn't even remember that he had a dog called Ivor at home who he adored. She was relieved to finally find a harmless-looking room where they could hopefully wait until whatever spell he had sprayed on himself wore off. If she had learned one thing about this strange land it was that most spells were short lived.

They found themselves in some sort of nursery where more dragons were softly singing to a room full of cots. Megan loved babies very much and decided that she was going to offer to volunteer for a while. She could also sing much better than the wailing group of dragon nursery assistants that sounded more like they could give babies nightmares than sweet dreams. However first she had to deal with Sabe who was looking around the room and muttering to himself.

'Sabe, I think you need to sleep this spell off,' she told him firmly and took the side down of an empty cot. 'In you go!' she ordered him and pushed him firmly inside.

He was rather big for it so she bent his legs up and tucked a few blankets around him. She was relieved that he didn't show any resistance. The Sabe she knew would have put up quite a fight at being tucked into a cot like a baby.

'Now just close your eyes and get some sleep. I'll come and get you in a bit.' She then wound the musical mobile that was suspended over the cot up and left him gazing at some sheep circling slowly round over his head. She wandered over to one of the dragons. Hopefully they were the sort of staff that liked to gossip too. She would be sure to find out as much as she could about the way the academy was run and hopefully someone would have heard about Marley, their longest residing student.

'Excuse me,' she interrupted the squawking lullaby. 'I'm here to volunteer. I know lots about babies. We have a few of them in our family and I can help you look after them.'

The dragons looked up at her and nodded. She started to sing a few lullabies that she knew from back home and was pleased when the dragons let her lead the songs as they tried to hum along with her. She couldn't wait to peep at the babies once they had stopped fidgeting under their blankets. Later when they had woken up, she hoped to be able to play games and cuddle them. After a few songs the babies were still fidgeting, so Megan decided to try and pat one of them to see if that helped.

'There there, little one. No wonder you can't settle with the blanket right over your head.'

She pulled the blanket back a little and was shocked to see not a baby but an egg. A huge green speckled egg that was rocking from side to side. She went to the next cot and there was another egg in there under a blanket, the same as the first only cracked down the side. She rushed around the nursery from cot to cot and every single one contained an egg in various stages of hatching. She felt very disappointed. She watched as one of the eggs hatched before her eyes and a small dragon stepped out. The nursery assistants gathered around and one of them lifted it up to get a closer look and shook her head. Another pointed out the dragon's furry tail and whiskers.

'Not dragon enough!' she remarked and promptly shoved it under her arm as it squawked and wriggled. 'I'll put it out the back. Can you change the bed-sheets and we'll get it ready for another one?' she asked Megan.

'But where are you taking it?' said Megan who was appalled. 'It's only just been born.' 'Well it can't stay here,' replied the nursery assistant. 'It's no good. It will learn to fend for itself in no time. Don't worry it won't starve. There's plenty of bins out there for it to find food until it's strong enough to make its own way.'

Megan looked at the baby dragon who was trying to adjust its eyes to the light as it was taken away leaving Megan open mouthed. The nursery assistant was back in a few minutes and told Megan off for not changing the sheets yet. Megan glanced over to the cot where she had left Sabe, and he appeared to be fast asleep. She had no choice but to remain in the nursery and watch the proceedings. One after another, the eggs hatched and were inspected. Those that were deemed dragon enough were allowed into the playroom next door, and those that were deemed inferior were taken away and placed outside the back door. She was so relieved when finally, she heard an angry roar from Sabe's cot. The nursery staff suddenly looked very excited.

'That's a proper gamalite if ever I heard one!' said the head nursery nurse and a crowd of them rushed over to see Sabe jump over the cot bars.

'Megan!' he yelled. 'You wait until I get you! How dare you put me in here!'

Megan ran over.

'Quick Sabe we need to get out of here! You were under some sort of spell where you lost your memory. I had no choice but to let you sleep it off!' She grabbed hold of his arm. 'We need to run!' she said and pulled him towards the door.

'You wicked children!' shouted one of the dragons. 'You just wait until we tell your teachers about this. We've had enough of you pranking us! It's the third time this week!' but Sabe and Megan were too fast for them. Out of the door they ran and up a flight of stairs where they joined a crowd of students and followed them into a classroom.

Chaos at The Palace

Back at the palace Amy was enjoying a pre dinner drink with Queen Augustine. She had decided that the queen was actually okay once you got to know her. If you looked beyond the over-the-top clothes and snappy finger gestures she was just like one of the bossier, know-it-all girls at her school. The queen was asking her if she had any pets. Amy had lots back home and she was telling the queen all about them. The queen listened enthusiastically.

'My parents were always great animal lovers. Many years ago, my sisters and I had lots of pets of our own: horses, dogs, cats... It was my father that trained the birds and the rabbits to do the jobs they do now.'

Amy swirled her drink around in its glass which seemed to have tiny fish swimming around in it.'

'So, what happened to your family?' she asked.

'Don't look so worried. They will dissolve in a minute and turn into sweets. They pop when you drink them. They're lovely.'

The queen laughed at Amy's worried face and continued,

'Well that's what I can't remember. One day we were preparing for our little sister's birthday party. I remember she was going to get her very own unicorn and she was so excited.

My next memory is riding with High Hat in the carriage towards the old lands. He was crying and so distraught. He promised me one day he would make everything better again but then he was gone too. In the years that followed I was never left alone. I was given everything I ever asked for, I was shown every corner of this kingdom and every beautiful thing it has to offer. It was like I was kept busy with no time to think about them, but I would often wake in the night and lay awake for hours vowing to come home and find my family. One day when I was old enough, they brought me back and that's when I met you and I knew at once that your higher powers can help put the missing pieces together.' Her eyes were shining with excitement. Amy took a deep breath.

'I will do everything I can to help you Queen Augustine but I'm not an enchantress. I'm not even a slight bit wizard or witch. I'm just a girl. I heard you are a pure blood wizard yourself. Can't you use some of your own powers to find out what happened?' The queen put her drink down abruptly.

'Don't you think I've tried?' she said. 'The thing with wizards is that their magic works best when they are together. One wizard on their own can only do the most basic of spells unless they have been specially trained. I asked High Hat if I can train at the academy, but he wouldn't hear of it. He always was overly protective of all of us. That's part of the problem. He would never let us out of his sight. He took his guardian duties very seriously.'

'Marley has the same problem with him,' said Amy. 'Did you ever have a brother?' The queen mouthed Marley's name to try and recall if she had heard of him.'

'No, no brothers. Just two very wonderful, if annoying at times, sisters. An older one and a younger one. You're very modest, aren't you? You're the most powerful enchantress I've ever met!'

'I am?' asked Amy. Now she was puzzled.

'Yes' said the queen 'Have you not noticed how you made the flowers and plants bloom the minute you arrived. You have the power to bring everything back to life, even the magic box, look!'

She pulled Ben's mobile phone out of her pocket and showed her. Sure enough it was now lit up and showing was the home screen with the club badge of Ben's favourite football team. Amy took the phone from the queen and started to look through it.

'There's no signal though,' she said, and she was somewhat disappointed. All she wanted to do was search to see if it was possible for her to suddenly develop magical powers.

'But look what it can do!' said the queen and showed her the camera function. 'I have imprisoned myself in it lots of times already, watch!' She then made Amy watch as she posed with various faces and took photos of herself.

'I never saw anything quite as magical as this box of yours.'

'No I don't think I ever have either,' lied Amy and the queen was pleased. She looked directly at her.

'Find my parents and sisters for me now! I command you!'

'But what if I can't?' said Amy.

'Of course your can! If you won't I will put you, that brother and that servant of yours into the dungeon and then I can ask my uncle High Hat to decide what to do with you.' Her face changed suddenly and she started to cry.

'I'm sorry. Please help me Enchantress Amy. I am desperate. You are my last hope.'

Amy put her arm around the queen and the queen began to

sob on her shoulder. She felt sorry for her and tried to imagine how she would feel if her own parents and siblings suddenly disappeared leaving her to grow up without them. The thought made her fearful and although part of her wanted to leave the palace as soon as she could she also felt she had to do try and help in some way. She thought hard as the queens' tears drenched her shoulder.

Eventually the queen stopped crying and composed herself. She sat up, poured another drink and snapped her fingers.

'Whatever is that brother of yours doing anyway? He should be bringing our starters up at any minute!'

Ben had started off very confidently. In his celebrity restaurant he had become very used to organising large teams of staff to produce wonderful dishes for fussy customers every night. A meal for two people should have been something he could do with his eyes closed.

When he first stepped into the kitchen he was greeted by a smart line of pixies, elves and young wizards in white aprons and hats who bowed and then nudged each other giggling. Their eyes were wide and keen and they looked a little nervous.

'I told you he would come!' whispered one very excited pixie to her friend next to her. 'I've got drawings of him all over my bedroom walls! One day I'm going to work at his restaurant too!'

The other elf laughed 'He would never work with you. I'm much more talented than you are! I can even make eggs on toast!' This comment was met with mutterings of doubt from the others and loud whispers of 'Who does she think she is? As if she can make egg on toast!' Ben asked them to be quiet so that he could look around and many sets of eyes followed him as he walked around the kitchen, marvelling at the vast space, the marble- topped counters and the neat lines of copper pots, pans and every gadget his could imagine laid out for him. He opened up huge storerooms full of fresh produce and flavours and walked up and down thinking how easy this was going to be. He had so many helpers too. He would hardly have to touch anything himself.

'Right then, let's get to work. First we are going to make a soup!' The announcement was met with faces of disgust and confusion.

'A what?' went a whisper among them.

'You know a soup. It's a traditional starter in most restaurants. You have it with bread rolls,' said Ben and there were no looks of recognition at his description but there was much shaking on heads.

'Don't worry, you will love it. This one is made from fresh tomatoes and peppers. You miss,' he instructed the elf who had proclaimed herself the most talented. 'Can you get me some of your finest tomatoes and a selection of fresh herbs?'

The elf promptly went very pale and fainted and the others gathered round her and lifted her onto some sacks of flour in the corner.

'Is she okay?' asked Ben who was rather taken aback.

'It's the excitement,' explained one of the wizards. 'It's not every day you get to meet a celebrity, especially one you have a huge crush on. She'll be fine in a bit.'

'Oh,' said Ben. He had temporarily forgotten the effect he had had on the customers at his restaurant, he'd had security guards back then. Maybe he should have brought a few along with him today? Never mind, it was too late for all that. A pixie tapped his elbow and held out a napkin and pen.

'It's for my mother,' he said. 'It would mean so much to her.'

Ben awkwardly signed the napkin and decided to collect the ingredients himself. He went to the storeroom and emerged with a huge basket of ripe vegetables and handfuls of fresh herbs. He spread the recipe page out on the table to show his assistants the picture of the soup. There was more giggling.

'It's red!' remarked one of them. 'It looks like one of the spells from Mr Quick Quack's Emporium. Is it the fire spell on toast?'

'No, it's tomato soup, made with fresh tomatoes and herbs. Where are the tomatoes?'

'They have been turned into liquid.'

'Oh, they will never allow that!' The group began shaking their heads in agreement and folding their arms in protest.

'Of course they will! First, I am going to boil them in water and then when I've removed the skins, I will whisk them up and turn them into liquid.'

Ben got out a large saucepan and placed it on the hob, picked up a tomato and then shouted loudly as something sharp and pin like went into his hand. He looked down in astonishment just as he saw small razor like teeth withdraw back into the tomato's skin.

'I don't believe it! That tomato just bit me!' He held his wounded hand to his chest as the tomato in question rolled out of his hand and jumped off the table, promptly followed by the other tomatoes that he had just gathered from the storeroom. They rolled in a line towards the sink and began to ascend like mountaineers until they reached the window frame and open window. They were quickly followed by hordes of other vegetables from the storeroom. One of the male elves stepped forward and told him.

'Can't blame them really. They were looking forward to being part of famous toast dishes and then they hear that they have been conned into becoming something called soup, they are insulted,' muttered one of the pixies.

'Hey you come back! shouted Ben at the vegetables. 'Change of plan! Tomatoes on toast sounds do able!' He ran towards the window and confidently grabbed a few handfuls of stubborn tomatoes which promptly launched themselves at his face where they went splat right on his nose. Tomato juice squirted all over him and forced him to close his eyes. The little kitchen attendants began to roar with laughter.

'Too late Sir Ben! They don't believe you!' And they laughed louder.

Ben was felt cross and humiliated. He was not going to be shown up by a parade of stuck-up vegetables. He was the lands greatest chef, and they were going to do what they were supposed to do, which was provide food for hungry people. People who by now were waiting with high expectations in the palace dining room. Wiping tomato juice from his eyes, he grabbed a few escaping red peppers and held them down on the worktop while he chopped them in half quickly, he then did the same with some of the tomatoes and onions, and ripped some of the herbs into pieces as they did their best to climb the curtains.

'Now let's see you escape!' he laughed as he took the chopped-up vegetables to show his assistants. As he proudly placed the chopping board down in front of them there were gasps of horror and many sets of hurt and frightened eyes looked at him as if they were worried they would be next. There was a strange long silence before one of them spoke.

'You've killed them!'

'Well, technically not, because they weren't actually alive and also how else am I supposed to cook if I can't chop up my ingredients?' There was a mutter of disbelief from the little people.

'Of course they were alive you clumsy clot! They can bite and run, what other proof do you need?' Ben wanted to joke that maybe they were some type of zombie vegetables, but the mood didn't seem right somehow.'

'Why didn't you just tell them what to do? There was no need to attack them with knives and boiling water.'

'You're not even a chef are you? You can't cook anything!' shouted one of the elves angrily.

'Of course I can cook! I'm a professional chef! I can just make toast then and we can put some new toppings on for the queen to try.' He had already dropped the idea of cooking anything from his recipe books at home. If these people wanted toast, then toast they could have.

He was going to do exactly what he had done in his restaurant and that was to sit back in a chair and tell his assistants exactly what to do.

'Right, now can you all collect me some bread and some butter? I have a brand new idea for a dish!' There was a sudden buzz of excitement.

'Now who wants to be the one to collect my special new topping?'

The assistants jumped up and down excitedly.

'Pick me! Pick me!' they cried in excitement. Ben looked at them all and decided to choose a small, elderly elf at the back that was almost getting trampled under the enthusiastic boots of the younger people.

'Would you like to be my special assistant?' he asked, and

the old man grinned from ear to ear to be of help.

The younger elves busied themselves collecting fresh bread from the storeroom and Ben directed them how to light the fire in the huge range cooker and use the toasting forks to get the bread nice and golden brown. He was so pleased with his idea for a new twist on his menu he was surprised he hadn't thought of it before. The queen would be absolutely delighted with his genius. He might even get a knighthood if he played his cards right. Excitedly, he whispered the secret ingredient to the old elf who could barely contain his surprise as he nodded and scurried off to collect what was needed.

Ben was far more relaxed now. This was so much easier that messing about with vegetables and following someone else's written instructions. He asked one of the pixies to go up to the dining room and get him a nice glass of pop while he relaxed in an armchair next to the range and called instructions to his team. He ordered them to use the best silver serving dishes, garnished with flowers from the garden. He took a sip of pop. To think it could have gone so horribly wrong had he tried those ambitious written recipes. He had definitely saved the day with his quick thinking and gained the respect of his team that had for a moment started to doubt him.

'Come on Old Mr Sign-A-Lot,' called the pixie who had fainted earlier making strange hand gestures to the old elf who was running in from the garden with a huge grin on his face. It was a strange name for the old elf Ben thought. He imagined the elf must have made painted signs prior to working at the palace. Sign-A-Lot carried the special ingredients with the greatest of care, and from his chair in the corner of the room, Ben watched him arrange the special new topping on each slice of bread, observing with pride the open mouths of the fascinated assistants.

'Now just hold the bread for a while in front of the fire so the toppings melt a little. That's it, brilliant. Now carry them all over here, place them on the silver plates, and I think we are ready to present our new dish to the queen. Well done everyone!' His team looked relieved and Sign-A-Lot was proud to be the one to carry the new dish over to Ben to take up to the dining room. Another of the pixies sounded the dinner gong. Ben lifted up the silver dome to observe his creation and immediately dropped the lid on the floor with a clang.

'Bees on toast!' he said in horror. Sign-A-Lot nodded proudly. On the toast swarmed hundreds of bees, they were very sticky with butter and very hot and bothered after being toasted by the fire.

'Cheese! I said cheese on toast! Did you not hear what I said?'

'Well obviously not you silly boy,' said one of the team 'Sign-A-Lot is deaf and if you expect him to lip read you are a very ignorant person.'

'What's the hold up?' shouted a familiar voice and Amy appeared at the top of the stairs. 'You had better bring that up because Queen Augustine is getting really impatient!'

'There's been a bit of a mix up,' said Ben. 'Get her to wait a bit longer. I just need to...' but his explanation was stopped by the bees rising up angrily from the toast and swarming around his kitchen assistants. They screamed and slapped them away with their hands, but they refused to remain in the kitchen a moment longer. They ran off, dropping the silver tray and the toast and trampling everything underfoot in the rush to escape. Ben had no assistants, a kitchen with food up the windows and on the floor, and no dish to present to the queen.

'Just ten more minutes Amy!' he shouted, trying to salvage toast that didn't have shoe imprints on and place it back onto the plate. Amy uttered a sigh of annoyance and turned to walk away.

'You've got ten minutes!' she shouted. 'Or we are never going to be allowed home!'

The Accidental Discovery of the Land of Childhood

Marley was having a wonderful time playing hide-and-seek in the enormous maze with Luna and Tip, even though he was losing. The pair of them found him very easily. Tip had the advantage that she could climb to the tops of the great hedges and get the best view of where the other two were. Luna on the other hand was as small and as light as a feather, and as soon as Marley caught a glimpse of her white dress or the side of her head and crept up on her, she was gone again and he would hear giggling from the other side of the maze. After a while he was thirsty, so called to Tip and Luna to have a break so they could head to the kitchen and ask Ben for some drinks. Tip bounced down immediately from above him and was soon at his heels remarking on the heat.

Luna did not show up. They walked about the paths winding and turning, following the sound of her laughter and calling her.

She was definitely around somewhere, they could hear her feet on the gravel and she called to them enthusiastically. 'Marley over here! Come see what I found!' They ran towards where they thought her voice was coming from as she kept calling to them, one minute sounding so close, the next so far away. Whatever she had found she was very excited about as her calls became more insistent. Finally, they came to the end of the maze, or it could have been the centre, they had walked so far through it. Marley followed Tip as he ducked through a low archway cut into the hedge, tall enough for a small child to fit through, and they found themselves in a wide courtyard with an elaborate stone pond and a fountain in the centre. Above the fountain was an expensive-looking sculpture of a group of children, holding hands in a circle and happily dancing about. Luna was standing transfixed on the wall surrounding the pond, pointing at the water. Marley and Tip ran up to her.

'Come down Luna, we don't want you to fall in, do we?' Marley couldn't see the bottom of the pond. As beautiful as it was it did look rather deep. Tip was standing back from it and looked horrified to see Luna so close to the water.

'Come here Luna, you are not allowed near the fountain!' she called nervously from the edge of the courtyard. Luna turned to look at them both and began to walk around the wall of the pond.

'It's so lovely Marley!' she bent over and let her hands touch the water 'It's warm!' she called out in surprise.

'Come down now Luna!' called Marley who was also feeling nervous at seeing her perched on the edge of the pond. 'Come down or I will put an ice spell on you so you won't be able to move until I defrost you!' At this Luna squealed with laughter like it was part of a game.

'I want an ice spell! I want to be an ice-cream!' she said as she jumped up and down in excitement.

'Right, that's it! Tip, help me out!' he asked as he raised his arms towards Luna. As he started to chant Luna turned to look at him, smiled, and promptly jumped into the fountain.

Marley froze in shock and then his survival instinct took over. He rushed to the side of the pool and glanced into the water. It was so deep. There was nothing to be seen of Luna, nothing to suggest that a few seconds ago she had been there other than large ripples flowing outwards. He turned to Tip.

'Get Ben now!' he shouted and Tip started to run back into the maze. Marley instinctively jumped straight into the fountain to save her and in a second, he too was below the surface.

Marley opened his eyes expecting to feel the sting and the blur as they adjusted to the water. Instead, his feet made contact with a hard floor. He opened his eyes. He was not in water but on dry land. He looked above and there was blue sky and sun. The fountain was nowhere to be seen. He was overwhelmed and happy to see Luna was in front of him sitting on the grass making a daisy chain. She looked up and waved. Marley looked up again. He needed to let Tip know somehow that the panic was over and Luna was safe but he couldn't figure out how to get back. Luna would know, he was sure. She had more magical knowledge than he did.

They were in a meadow of bright green grass strewn with wildflowers. It was the most beautiful of summer days and set out on the grass was a picnic with all his favourite food. There was even food that he had never tried before but he instinctively knew what it tasted like and that he loved it. Luna was now arranging dolls, teddies and groups of toy figures around the picnic blanket as if they were guests. Among them Marley could see a smartly dressed soldier figure, the type he would have liked for himself. He wondered if it belonged to anyone and whether he could possibly take it home with him.

'But Luna! Where did you get all these toys?' he asked her in amazement. Luna pointed to a nearby tree and in its branches, Marley could see the most incredible tree-house accessed by a sturdy rope ladder.

He went to hug her for he was overcome with happiness that she was safe but she wriggled free from his grasp and told him to get off as she was trying to get the tea ready. Leaving her to her game and convinced this was some sort of good dream, Marley climbed up the tree house ladder and could hardly believed what he found there. There was a comfy hammock and a huge telescope pointing out of the window towards the sky. Marley had always longed for a telescope and a den of his own, and this one was just like the ones he had dreamed of for himself. He peeked through the telescope. It was too light to look at the night sky so he pointed it as far into the distance as he could.

'Luna! Luna! Look I can see toy-shops and they are open. Let's go and have a look around.'

He climbed down the ladder and had to literally pull Luna away from her game. He wasn't sure how to get to the shops exactly, but he didn't have to think about it for long as approaching them slowly came an enormous toy train on a track that he somehow hadn't noticed before. Now he knew he must be dreaming.

'Luna, is there any way we can get a message to Tip and the others to let them know we are safe and that you didn't drown?' Luna looked at him and smiled her usual smile like she was half laughing at him.

'She already knows,' Luna said and she sounded very certain of it.

'How could she know? She just saw you jump into a deep fountain. We were both so frightened.'

'No Marley. You thought I was going to drown. Tip didn't.' Marley remembered how Tip had stayed well back from the fountain and how she had nervously told Luna to get down. He wasn't so sure.'

'I promise she knows,' said Luna and persuaded him to climb back into the tree house and look through the telescope. In the distance Marley could see Tip at the edge of the maze playing with the invisibility cloak they had discarded earlier. She was rolling about in it until finally it worked its magic and Tip was gone.

'That cat is a nuisance sometimes,' said Marley. 'It's a good job there wasn't a real emergency, fat lot of use she would have been.' He stepped away from the telescope. Ben would be busy in the kitchens and Amy would be busy talking to the queen. He smiled a huge smile.

'Hey Luna, do you reckon we have a bit more time before we need to find the others?' Luna nodded excitedly and they both knew they were going to have a great time.

They jumped on the train as the whistle blew and off they went towards the toy-shops, marvelling as the beautiful countryside passed by.

'Look at how clear that lake is!' shouted Marley as they passed a beautiful shallow lake. 'I bet even you could swim safely there Luna!' They both pressed their noses against the window and were amazed to see the lake was surrounded by colourful water-slides, some looped and some straight. Marley desperately hoped that the lake was not an illusion like the fountain had been for he was definitely coming back here as soon as he could, and he was going to bring the others with him.

They arrived at a village square surrounded with shops and jumped off at the station. A balloon-seller dressed as a clown was standing outside, his collection of colourful balloons blowing gently against the sky.

'Excuse me, where is this place?' asked Marley.

'The Land of Childhood of course!' said the clown and offered them each a free balloon. *The Land of Childhood*, Marley thought to himself. Luna was pulling him towards a fancy dress shop with bright lights in the windows. Inside was every type of costume you could imagine. Luna was so excited and pulled one of the costumes off the rails, then another and ran about with armfuls of them, until Marley had to tell her to slow down. The shop assistant, rather than telling her off, seemed to be encouraging her, sharing her enthusiasm as Luna paraded as an astronaut, then a firefighter and finally as a fluffy dog with large ears.

Once he had seen that dressing up was encouraged, he had a great time trying on the costumes too.

'Look Luna, who am I?' Marley called to her as he strutted up and down the shop in a chef's hat and apron with his hands on his hips. Luna laughed out loud and joined in the game, now dressed in a golden crown and long purple robes she was snapping her fingers in the air shouting. 'Everyone must do as I say! I am your Queen!'

Sometime later they ran out of the shop having been allowed to keep their favourite items on. Luna was dressed as a fairy combined with a mechanic's steel-capped boots and a circus master's top hat and Marley was a racing car driver, complete with a personalised helmet.

Next stop was a whirlwind race around the toy shop as they filled their trolleys with all the toys they had ever wanted, re-membering to buy what the others might like too as souvenirs: toy cars, bubble machines, water pistols, pirate ships, tea sets and all types of soft toys. They had no idea how they would take the large items home but the keen shopkeeper, obviously delighted to have plenty to do, said he would package them up and send them on to the cottage on their behalf.

As they walked out of the shop with their bags of toys, sweets and clothing, the clock in the square began to chime.

'We should be getting back to the palace, Luna. We absolutely have to bring the others here for a day out. Wait until they hear about this place! Do you have any idea how to get us back?'

Luna nodded-a little reluctantly, and clapped her hands. A small wooden tricycle and a mountain bike appeared from around the corner and wheeled themselves over to them.

'We ride back?' asked Marley, hanging the bags over the handlebars. He jumped on. 'I'll follow you, Luna.'

Soon they were off riding away from the shops and along quiet peaceful country lanes. Marley had possibly had the best day of his life. He was seriously considering applying for a gardening or kitchen assistant job at the palace. Imagine if he could spend all his lunch breaks here? They rode on through the winding lanes and Marley's legs were soon getting tired. He began to yawn as Luna rode into the distance.

'Wait for me!' he called after her. 'Please don't let this be just a dream.'

More Discoveries

Sabe and Megan, meanwhile, were doing their best to blend into the crowds of academy students at the back of a very noisy classroom. Swarms of trainee wizards and witches were fighting for places at the back too, no one wanted to be at the front. They were shouting, elbowing and pushing each other out of the way and chairs were falling over as they argued over seats.

'What's the difference between a wizard and a witch anyway?' whispered Sabe. 'I mean some of the boys are witches and some of the girls are wizards. How do they decide?'

A pinched face girl turned and stared at them as if they were ridiculous.

'You mean you don't even understand the difference? What part of the land did you crawl out from?'

The tone of her voice soon caught the attention of the other students who laughed and threw books at them. A tall arrogant looking boy walked up to them.

'I'll show you! Everyone starts off here learning the basics- then, they choose their specialism. For example, witches specialize in cures and magical potions mostly.' He took a tub out of his pocket and opened the lid. The other students crowded around Megan and Sabe, listening keenly with grins on their faces. 'This is one I made earlier.' He then took out a pinch of powder and flicked it over Sabe. 'Here's a beauty spell to make your eyelashes and hair lovely and long.' The students began to laugh as Sabe's hair was suddenly a mass of curls trailing on the floor.

'Change it back!' he shouted and stood up so he was level with the laughing boy. Megan was shocked to see Sabe with such dramatic hair and eyelashes.

'All right Rapunzel, keep your hair on,' he muttered and took out another pinch of powder, this time from a second compartment in the tub. He blew it in Sabe's face, and his hair and eyelashes began to immediately shrink back, much to his relief. The boy then walked round to Megan's side of the desk. 'And wizards specialize in words that have remarkable effects, known better as spells.' He crouched down so he was level with Megan's face. 'You do know what a spell is don't you?' he laughed, tapping her on the head with his wand.

'Of course I do!' said Megan. 'Sabe and I were just discussing which area we want to specialise in...'

She was forced to stop as she was not able to finish her sentence. She looked at Sabe, or what had been Sabe, as he was now an owl sporting chunky brown feathers, huge round eyes and a tiny beak. Megan looked down at the claws where her feet had been and then up at the desk which was now towering above her. As much as she liked owls, she had never had any desire to be one. She looked angrily at the boy and Sabe jumped up onto the desk and pecked his hand. The boy screamed and threatened to leave them like that until dinner-time.

The classroom door opened and in swept Miss Whizzity, clip-board and wand in hand. The students raced to sit down, leaving Sabe and Megan hidden at the back, looking at each other, neither were able to speak.

'Now class,' boomed Miss Whizzity as she stood behind her desk and silence fell across the room. 'I hope you have all memorised your spell books as we will first be having a random chant test.'

She began to hand out textbooks and pens. 'You know how it works. I start with the name of a spell and you write the whole thing out except for the final line.' There were groans of boredom from the class who clearly preferred the practical side of learning. She stopped suddenly when she reached the back row and saw Sabe and Megan sitting on the chairs, their beaks and eyes level with the edges of the desks. They involuntarily rotated their heads on their necks full circle to avoid looking at her.

'Who brought these familiars into the classroom?' she shrieked in surprise and quickly opened the window as she began clapping her hands and trying to shoo them away. Sabe and Megan looked at each other and wobbled from side to side in an attempt to fly away. Neither of them had a clue how to use their wings so they remained there shuffling on their clawed feet and flapping their wings without being able to take off. The other students laughed.

'Ah, they have just been summoned I see. Well, they will work it out for themselves sooner or later,' sighed Miss Whizzity. 'Right class, ignore them, turn to the contents list on page four, now complete this spell...'

As she clip clopped to the front of the class on her heeled boots there was a sob from one of the students at the front.

'I want to go home! I'm going to behave in future. I didn't want to come here!' Miss Whizzity looked a bit panicky as she bent over the girl who now had her head on the desk and was crying.

'Nonsense you are going to be one of our most powerful graduates!' She tapped her on her head, whispered something, and the girl suddenly sat up straight.

'Now do you still want to go home?' The girl shot Miss Whizzity a puzzled look.

'Why would I want to go home? I want to be part of the magic revolution!' She then looked around at her shocked classmates and mouthed, *'what is she on about?'*

'That's more like it. Now someone tell me the opening lines for the spell to turn a stubborn person into an ant?'

There was another protest from the other side of the room.

'I don't feel well, Miss. I can't remember getting here? My parents will be worried.'

Miss Whizzity rushed over to the boy who was talking and began to tap him on the head. 'Feeling better?' she asked. The boy looked up at her. 'I feel fine. Why shouldn't I?'

Megan and Sabe looked at each other but still couldn't speak. They needed to get out of the room. Miss Whizzity asked someone to get High Hat. 'The Memory Breaker Spell must be wearing off,' she muttered. 'Those laundry staff are useless!'

There was more unease in the classroom as one by one the students seemed to come out of whatever trance they were in and started to ask where they were and why they were there. The boy who had turned Megan and Sabe into owls turned to look at them and his face was softer and full of concern.

'Get help!' he whispered and stroked them quickly on the head with his wand before Miss Whizzity strolled towards him.

Sabe and Megan's feet began to rise from the chairs and they began to fly, very clumsily at first, as they circled the room and nearly crashed into a few wall displays. They quickly got the hang of it and swooped out of the window. Sabe followed Megan as she flew around the academy roofs looking for the nursery and where the rejected baby gamalites could be. After a while she saw the bins and their small outlines trying to scavenge around them looking for something to eat. She dipped downwards, Sabe following close behind; she was going to wait with them until the spell wore off and she and Sabe could be themselves again. They had a lot to discuss and a lot of gamalites to rescue.

Marley and Luna rushed into the castle kitchens in excitement.

They had ridden until they found themselves at the fountain in the maze where their whole adventure had started. The fountain walls were solid as they had propped their bikes up against them. Marley placed his hand in the water and saw it was definitely wet. Had he and Luna really jumped in and emerged completely dry? It had been the most bizarre but amazing time and he couldn't wait to tell the others and try to take them to the Land of Childhood.

There were bees buzzing everywhere in the kitchen, and Ben was busy trying to lift them off plates of toast with a spoon where they had got their legs stuck in butter.

'Cheese on toast! I said cheese on toast!' he was nearly crying in frustration as his assistants stood awkwardly around him shaking their heads. He looked up when he saw them.

'Help me please! Do you have any magic you can use that can fix this mess?'

Marley nodded, keen to prove his newfound talent for spells. He grabbed some empty plates, raised his arms over them and started to chant.

'*Free the bees and give us some cheese.*'

Luna gave him a playful nudge in the ribs.

'Boring cheese on toast!' she teased. 'That's a silly spell Marley, let me do it' She passed

her hand over the line of empty plates.

'*Jelly on toast, ice cream on toast,*
Brownies and cupcakes and things we love most,
This is the twist that will make the queen smile,
And get Ben a knighthood for his cool menu style.
Best of all make it calorie free,
And safe for our teeth, and safe for the bee!

Toast began to appear on each plate topped with every

puddings they could imagine.   Luna looked delighted and Marley was proud of her.

'Won't that toast ruin the taste of the desserts though?' asked Ben as everyone in the kitchen leaned forward to marvel at the elaborate display before them.

'No, the toast isn't real, look,' said Luna and poked her finger through it to show everyone it was just an illusion. 'The desserts are though!' she reassured them and then put her finger in a chocolate éclair to show them. She licked her finger and smiled in approval. 'This is yummy.'

There was a shout from the corridor outside.

'Ben why are you taking so long! Queen Augustine is getting so hungry she's starting to get cross!'

'We're bringing the food up right now,' called Ben with obvious relief and he instructed everyone to carry a plate up to the dining room.

'Erm, where do you think you're going?' he asked Luna. 'You're not supposed to be here remember!' Luna looked briefly disappointed before shouting, 'My invisibility cloak! I left it somewhere in the garden! I'll be up in a minute!' and with that she ran back outside.

This really is the most incredible food I have ever seen or tasted remarked Queen Augustine as she whipped her phone out of her pocket for the fifth time to take yet more photos of herself holding various desserts up to her mouth. The first time she had done this, Ben immediately recognised his missing phone and nudged Amy hard.

'That's mine!' he whispered and looked accusingly at Amy. 'What is she doing with it?' Amy shrugged and pretended to be interested as the queen scrolled through numerous photos of herself posing in various locations in the palace. Under the vast dining table, and hidden under the invisibility cloak at Marley's feet, Luna rolled her eyes. She thought the queen was behaving in the most ridiculous manner. Every time Marley secretly passed her some of his dessert to try, she made a point of poking her head out of the cloak so he could see her and impersonating her by pulling faces in a way that made Marley laugh. He kept having to hide his amusement by putting yet another spoonful of strawberry jelly into his mouth.

'Is there something funny?' the queen asked Marley, who was now trying so hard not to laugh he was almost the same colour as the jelly. Unable to speak with his mouth full, Marley just shook his head quickly. The queen sighed and checked her appearance once again with the phones camera, pouting slowly as she did so and said to Amy, 'It is most unusual that allow your servant to eat with you. Still as you are doing me such a great favour today I will on this occasion turn a blind eye.' She sighed loudly. 'But will you please ask him to remove that helmet off the table? Dreadful manners,' she tutted and pouted at the phone again.

Marley removed his racing driver helmet, placed it back on his head and pulled the visor down. He had eaten quite enough of the desserts anyway and he could feel the sting in his eyes as tears started to form.

At least if he wore his helmet no one would see how sad he was. The queen had not even bothered to ask his name. Every time he had tried to contribute to the conversation, she had seemed to look through him as if he was irrelevant, before turning her attentions back to her important celebrity guests. It made him feel worthless and unwanted, which was the way he had always felt for as long as he could remember. Embarrassing, clumsy

Marley, always in the way, an unwanted responsibility. The thought made his eyes fill up and a tear began to slide down his cheek, which made his visor start to steam up.

He felt something brush his hand and looked down. Luna was gripping his hand firmly and stroking the top of it. Her kindness somehow made him cry harder. How he longed to wipe the smile off that spoiled queen's face. He sat in silence trying to whisper an elevation spell. If he could just anonymously tip one dessert over her, that would be a small victory, however Luna and Tip hadn't managed to show him how to do silent chants yet so despite his best attempt the spell attempt was not successful.

The queen was chatting enthusiastically about her travels to the old lands and how she would give Ben and Amy knighthoods so that they could travel there whenever they wanted and stay as her guest in any of her magnificent homes. Ben looked pleased but Amy looked worried.

'But I don't know how to find your parents. Can't you hire a detective? Do you have those here?' asked Amy. 'Or you could write to everyone in the land offering a reward for information leading to their discovery.'

The queen put down the phone finally and looked thoughtful.

'I have already tried all those things. I have spent money on the finest crystal balls, the cleverest problem-solving elves and every type of magic person I know around here but none of them come up with any answers.' She wasn't smiling anymore but twisting a napkin into tight shapes. 'But I know here in my heart,' she tapped her chest passionately, 'that my parents and sisters are alive and without family I am nothing. Like all who are born magical we can only make things happen when we are together. Strong magic only works when there is a team effort.' She stopped for a moment. 'Unless of course you are an enchantress like yourself or an enchanter like my uncle High Hat. Then of course you have enough power to make things happen without anyone's help.' She put her head in her hands. 'Without family I am nothing and I would swap all this wealth tomorrow to live with them in a cave!' She gripped Amy's hand and gave her a hopeful smile. Amy was feeling more uncomfortable by the minute.

Marley was confused. High Hat had certainly not seemed much of an enchanter when Luna suspended him from the ceiling and turned him into a mouse. He was aware of Luna fidgeting next to his legs, probably bored. It had been a long time for a small child to sit still. Then a sudden thought occurred to him. *What if Luna was an enchantress?* She had changed herself from a dragon into a girl, she had tied High Hat into knots, had created a feast in front of their eyes and could perform more spells than any of his fellow students at the academy. She had even found the Land of Childhood. It was certainly something he was going to discuss with Tip when she finally decided to show up from whichever part of the castle or grounds she was exploring. He decided to try and contribute to the conversation one more time.

'You could try looking for them in the Land of Childhood.' Everyone around the table stopped what they were doing and stared at Marley. The queen looked pale and shocked.

'Who told you about that place?' she demanded.

'No one,' said Marley. 'I found it by accident when I was looking round the garden and sort of fell into the fountain.' The queen stood up suddenly and looked desperately out of the window.

'That was our secret place. My sisters and I created it many

many years ago and no one knew about it – not even our parents. I have tried many times to return but now every time I jump in that fountain I just get wet and cold. I thought the land had gone.'

She embraced Amy. 'This is your doing I just know it. How can I ever thank you! I certainly will look there. I'm going right now! Everyone wait here. I won't be long.'

And with that she gathered up her skirts and ran from the room leaving everyone staring at each other. In a few minutes she was back excitedly as she grabbed the phone from Ben's hand and ran out again shouting, 'I must capture everything to show you.'

Once she was gone, Luna climbed out from under the table and unwrapped her invisibility cloak. 'It's boring under there can we go now?' she asked.

'Maybe we should just sneak off suggested Amy. 'Before she finds out that I can't be of much help to her.'

'We need to locate Tip first,' said Marley as Luna stood on a chair and indicated that she wanted him to give her a piggyback.

'And I want my phone back,' said Ben. 'Mother said she won't get me another one until Christmas and that's ages away. And I want to see this Land of Childhood place. It sounds fun. Sorry Amy you are stuck here for a bit.'

'Luna will take you there,' said Marley. 'I've decided I'm going to get Sabe and Megan back from the academy. Solving mysteries no longer matter. I've told Tip we can just move away and I'm going to get money working as an odd job wizard. There has got to be some part of this land that High Hat can't find us. Tip has agreed anyway.'

'No she hasn't,' said Luna quietly hoping that Marley would take note.

There was a rumbling sound as the china on the table rattled, the toast illusions started to fade and the few desserts that remained on top of them collapsed into sloppy messes. Luna dived quickly under the table as Queen Augustine was appeared back in the room. She was dressed as a soldier with a large stuffed dog and Marley's clothing under her arm and a balloon tied to her wrist.

'That was so much fun!' she declared. 'No more heavy dresses! I feel free!' She cuddled her toy dog and smiled. She handed Marley his clothes back which she had found in the fancy-dress shop changing room and told him to go and get his uniform back on. Marley was relieved to get his clothes back, but he walked out of the room sulkily. He wished someone would see him as someone important for a change. Regardless, he got dressed and went back into the room quickly, hoping to hear more about how the queen had got on in the Land of Childhood.

'That place hasn't changed a bit!' she was telling Amy. 'Even our tree house is still there. No one had seen my family though. What's your next idea?' She enthusiastically positioned herself next to Amy and took a photo of them together without asking her.

'Hey!' said Marley. 'It was my idea to look there not hers.' But the queen told him to be quiet.

'I don't have any more ideas,' said Amy. 'I'm sorry but I don't know where they are. Maybe you should ask High Hat. He seems to know a lot about what goes on round here.'

'He's been trying to find them all the time I've been gone,' said the queen. 'It's too close to home I suppose. It's his family too. We need an unrelated enchanter like yourself. You need to stop being so modest and just tap into your deepest powers.'

'I can't!' said Amy. 'I don't have any powers, I keep telling you! Where I come from, I've never needed to use any.'

'Nonsense!' said the queen. 'You can be my guest here for as long as it takes. Where is my family?' She began to raise her voice in desperation.

'Er, can I have my phone back now?' asked Ben and prised it from the queen's hands. The queen threw her toy dog across the room in a temper and popped the balloon with a fork.

'Enough of the niceties now,' she shouted. 'High Hat may not be able to help me but he certainly has enough spells to help Amy remember some of her magic. 'You,' she instructed Marley. 'Run along to the academy and bring me some Memory Breaker spells. Amy will soon remember the powers she was born with.' She snapped her fingers at him.

'Don't worry I was on my way there anyway!' He was only too glad to get out of the room. Once in the corridor he had to untangle Luna who was clinging onto his legs.

'Don't go there Marley!' she pleaded with him. 'It's not safe for you to be there on your own'

'I'm not on my own Luna,' he reassured her. 'I will have Sabe and Megan with me and I will borrow your cloak if that's okay?' He took the cloak from her and gave her a hug. 'Besides, I'm a much better wizard now. You taught me well remember?' And with that he began to walk towards the palace front door leaving Luna sitting on the floor.

'But I didn't teach you anything Marley,' she said, but it was too late, he was already gone.

The Great Rescue

Sabe and Megan had been doing their best to rummage through the bins to find food for the baby gamalites. With their half scales and half fur, they were clearly experiments that had somehow gone wrong, but what was it all for? They certainly had a few theories.

By evening the spell that had turned them into owls had worn off. The children were glad to be rid of their beaks and feathers and to finally be able to speak again.

'Why would anyone do this?' asked Megan. She was appalled at the way the animals had been discarded like rubbish. 'What will happen to them? How are they supposed to survive?'

She lovingly picked up a gamalite with a kitten's face that had been walking on its hind legs and trying to swat flies away with it's short scaly paws.

'Ouch!' said Megan and quickly dropped the gamalite as it roared at her and small flames flew out of its mouth, burning Megan's arm. It then ran away and hid under a bin where it peeked out at her warily.

'They will become feral quite soon,' said Sabe. 'I expect they just learn to fend for themselves.'

'But it's so wrong!' protested Megan.

'I know,' said Sabe. 'This sort of thing needs to be stopped.

This is what the Rainbow River rabbit meant when he told me about people using the higher magic in a selfish way. If High Hat can cross breed dragons until he works out how to create powerful monsters, as well as training up an army of witches and wizards to take over the kingdom there will be no stopping him.'

'But it's all fake,' said Megan. 'None of those students are here out of choice. They are under some sort of spell. There's something in that spray they use in the laundry that wipes their memories. That's what happened to you Sabe.' She stopped as he was indicating that she be quiet and they should hide. 'What is it?' she whispered.

'Someone's coming,' said Sabe and they backed away into the shadows behind the bins.

They watched as two hooded dark figures crept silently around the bins with nets and a large bag. One by one the gamalites were coaxed towards the figures with food they were holding out. Once they began to eat from the hand of one of the figures, then the second figure swooped in with a net and one by one the squawking gamalites were forced into the bag and the top was tied. After a while Megan could watch no longer. She jumped out of her hiding place to confront them.

'Stop! Release those gamalites now! They are only babies and you are mean to steal them when they can't fight back!'

She stopped and the figures removed their hoods so she could see their faces. They recognised her immediately.

'Megan? Is that you? What are you doing here?' Sabe poked his head out from where he was hiding and breathed a sigh of relief.

'Manny! Griff!' What are you doing here?'

'Rescuing baby gamalites of course!' said Manny and Griff

put down his net and went to steady Manny who looked almost weak with shock.

'We come when we can,' Griff explained. 'It's getting harder for Manny now, but even if we can save a few of them, it's something. How did you two get here and why are you wearing academy uniforms?'

Sabe and Megan sat down on the nearby wall with them. They fed the gamalites the treats Manny and Griff had brought, and explained exactly what they were trying to do, from finding out who Marley was to putting a stop to whatever High Hat was planning. Manny and Griff nodded their heads as if they already knew.

'High Hat has done some awful things' said Griff. We have been discussing ways to stop him for years but who would believe us? We would just get labelled a couple of crazy eccentrics. We need to convince Queen Augustine. She's the only one that can override him and close this place down but she's so young and naive. She believes everything he tells her.'

'And she is far too young to be a queen,' Manny said. 'She has no experience of life but a naive queen is exactly what High Hat wants. He can do what he likes, and she will never question it.'

'We can stop him though.' said Megan. 'Amy and Ben have made friends with Queen Augustine and I think she would listen to them. Is there any way to stop the spell that all these students are under?'

'The Memory Breaker spell?' said Manny. 'That's if you can get hold of it because no one knows where High Hat keeps it. Well, you would just give lots of it to whoever is affected by it, and it will work in reverse. You would need to find a way to administer it to them though without them knowing.'

Sabe and Megan looked at each other in delight. They knew where the Memory Breaker spells were kept, and they knew they just needed to spray it onto the students. There was a chance, a small but very real chance that they could do this and they excitedly told Manny and Griff all about it.

In his invisibility cloak, Marley had been strolling around the academy for quite a long time and he was very annoyed. He had seen the laundry rooms, the dragon nursery and even listened in on a few staff room meetings, and he had seen and heard all he needed. He had learned more about the academy in a few hours than he had in the century he had been a student there. After spending a long time watching the activity in the laundry and eavesdropping, he had located the Memory Breaker spell in the storeroom. He now carried a container of it as he looked, crossly, for the best way out of the building. The queen could have her silly Memory Breaker spell to try out on Amy and once she saw it didn't work, she would have to let them all go.

One thing he was now sure of, was that High Hat was absolutely no uncle of his. He wasn't even a relative. He was convinced that he, Marley, a half-human, half-wizard was some sort of experiment gone wrong like the gamalites were. The truth was he probably had never had parents. He had come straight out an egg or a test tube and into the academy. *Well, at least that was one mystery solved,* he thought as he continued to search for Sabe and Megan.

He eventually found them out the back of the nursery, casually chatting to Manny and Griff from the dragon sanctuary. He was so relieved to see them. He was going to tell them he wished to gather all his friends together and return to the cottage so that he, Tip and Luna could start packing ready for their new life. He was quite taken aback when they told him that wouldn't be possible as they were going to free all the academy students and tackle High Hat first. He banged the cannister down on the ground with annoyance.

'Look I just want to go home!' he protested. 'None of this matters any more. High Hat can do as he wants for all I care as long as I am far away from him.' No one was listening. They were too obsessed with looking at the can of Memory Breaker that Marley had just conveniently placed at their feet.

'Frank your magic really is something special,' remarked Manny. 'This is exactly what we have been talking about.'

'I'm not Frank,' said Marley. 'Why does everyone keep calling me Frank? By the way that familiar you gave me, the little dragon. She turned into a little girl but I'm keeping her anyway.' Manny and Griff chuckled.

'You really must be a very powerful wizard! We always knew she wasn't a full dragon but not even Manny's magic could have accomplished that,' said Griff. Marley was proud of the compliment. He was going to make good money as a jobbing wizard after all.

He didn't pay much attention as they came up with a plan. He was just delighted with how much he had progressed as a wizard. He decided to try out his powers on some of the gamalites. He lined up some of the more docile ones on the wall and tried to turn them back into full dragons. That didn't work so he then tried to create some more food for them by waving his arms over the scraps from the bins and imagining piles of fresh fruit instead. That didn't work either. Finally, he tried to summon a carriage drawn by crow chauffeurs so that they could at least have some sort of getaway vehicle if the plans went wrong and they needed to make a fast escape. Yet the skies were empty with not a bird in sight. It was as if all the magic he had recently learned had suddenly disappeared.

He kicked the ground in frustration and decided to try the most basic spell he could think of. A Shape-Shifting spell. He walked over to the smallest bin and started to chant at it. He thought it would be fun to turn it into a ball for the gamalites to play with. The bin shook slightly, took on a sightly rounder form and then began to roll across the courtyard, spilling out rotten food and bits of paper as it went as the others shouted at him to run after it and bring it back. He did, and as he struggled back with it there was no denying that it was most certainly still a bin.

Marley looked down at his hands. It didn't make sense. Why could he no longer perform even the most simple spell? He had seen the results of his own magic powers. Firstly at the talent show when Tip had been watching him proudly, then all those times when Luna had been with him, encouraging him and then clapping when he finally got the spells right. A thought suddenly came to him and it made him feel a bit embarrassed.

What if High Hat had been right all along and he would never be a wizard? What if he had never had any magic? What if Tip and Luna had been pretending he had all this time, to help his confidence when really it was them doing the spells to make him feel better.

He didn't like that thought at all. They probably laughed at him behind his back. No wonder they had gone quiet when he had suggested working as a jobbing wizard. He made up his mind to ask them if this was the case and tell them he didn't want their sympathy and help. If he had no magic, then there was nothing he could do about it but just learn to be himself and everyone else would just have to accept him how he was. But if he couldn't move away and make a new start with Tip and Luna and be a jobbing wizard there was only one other alternative. He would have to find a way to deal with High Hat.

'What do you want me to do in this grand plan then?' he asked.

The others were discussing the best way to get the Memory Breaker over the students quickly so that the spell could be reversed. The staff would have no chance of maintaining order once up against hundreds of rebelling students. He put his hands in his pockets and felt the outline of hard plastic. *The water pistols!* He still had the water pistols from The Land of Childhood! He looked at the cannister of Memory Breaker on the floor and quickly counted the water pistols. He had at least five of them on him.

'Everyone look!' he called. 'I've come up with a plan!'

'How many students do you think we can get?' asked Megan as she filled up her pistol with the spell.

'Just get whoever you can,' said Manny. We can take more supplies to the dining hall.

Then tell the ones who have regained their memories to bring the others here.'

'Do you think they will listen?' asked Sabe. 'They might just panic or run off.'

'They won't,' said Griff. 'They will remember everything up to the point they were brought here against their will and then they will want to help their friends.'

They decided to split up and cover different parts of the academy. Griff, it was decided would stay on the ground floor with Manny, who couldn't manage the stairs, and they would fill as many jugs from the kitchen as they could with

Memory Breaker to make sure everyone could re gain their memories. 'We will throw it over people if he have to,' said Manny confidently. Sabe, Megan and Marley would then take up different positions in the academy and walk through the corridors and rooms, squirting anyone they saw with their water pistols.

'What about the teachers and the dragon staff?' asked Megan. 'Should we get them too?' 'Most definitely worth a try,' said Manny and they all went to take up their positions.

They each ran quickly through their chosen floor. At first the students thought the children were fellow students who were misbehaving by initiating a water fight, and some of the more daring ones decided to get them back by casting spells to drench them with invisible buckets of water. It was great fun, even though the floors quickly became as slippery as ice which made running about quite difficult. Before long the students who had been covered in Memory Breaker would stop staring or fighting back and started to ask their friends where they were. Soon there were students crying, shouting, ripping their cloaks in half and stamping on their pointy hats as they were told to go to the dining room if they wanted to go home. Some of them did, but most of them stayed put, confused, and shouting for their parents.

On the top floor where Marley was, Miss Hagworth and Miss Whizzity had appeared and they were very cross indeed. They were even more cross when he squirted them in their faces with his water pistol. He had never really liked them much anyway and it was quite satisfying to see them shocked, speechless and soaked. He then quickly hid himself in a nearby cloakroom and listened to see what would happen.

Miss Whizzity soon began to cry and remembered that she had been enjoying her retirement after teaching for many years at a private school for fairies when High Hat had appeared on the door step and asked her for a cup of tea. She couldn't remember anything after that she sobbed to Miss Hegarty.

Miss Hegarty was drying herself on a towel she had summoned from the air and she was furious. She had been a private cookery teacher who baked cakes and sold them at the market when one day High Hat had appeared and asked her to appear in a new stage show and competition he was planning about the land's best bakers. She had naturally refused as she preferred a quiet life and before she could protest High Hat was popping up in every supermarket she ventured into, threatening to turn her famous cakes into worms. To keep him quiet she told him she would think about it. Then everything was a blur until suddenly she was here, right now, dressed in awfully boring clothes and shoes so sensible, she was embarrassed to be seen in them. She wanted to get back to her kitchen, her market stall and her elaborate silk scarf collection and she wanted to go right now. Marley crept out of his hiding place and tried to reason with them, grateful that neither of them seemed to recognise him from his days as the most hopeless trainee in the academy.

'Please come to the dining hall first!' he begged. You must help me rescue the other students that High Hat has tricked with Memory Breaker spell. I can't seem to round them up. Please help. You are both fantastic teachers and you will know what to do.'

Miss Hagworth and Miss Whizzity beamed knowingly at one another. Marley was relieved that neither of them mentioned the time when he'd only managed half the clothing makeover spell and left Miss Hagworth's underwear showing. They spoke to him like he was a helpful stranger.

'This way children,' the teachers called to the loud and chaotic crowds of students who were quickly recovering their memories. 'Everyone must assemble in the dining hall before we can go home! We will do a final registration.' The students, to Marley's relief, began to calm under the order of Miss Hegarty and Miss Whizzity and regardless of whether they had regained their memories or not were herded like sheep down the stairs and towards the dining hall.

On the lower floors Megan and Sabe raced through the laundry area, grabbing re-enforcements of Memory Breaking spray and squirting as many of the dragon assistants as they could. They weren't expecting much to happen. but they quickly stopped their work and pulled off their aprons.

'About time we had a holiday, ladies!' shouted one who could speak. 'Who remembers those times in Holiday Land when we were young enough to stay up all night?'

The others nodded at each other enthusiastically as they scrambled for the door. Sabe and Megan ran quickly towards the nursery determined to save as many baby dragons as they could.

They burst through the door and interrupted yet another awful lullaby that the dragons were trying to sing.

'I should get you for crimes against music!' Megan called and squirted the lot of them. Sabe and Megan then crouched behind a cot and waited to see what would happen.

'Babies!' called one of the dragons in delight. 'So many babies here! Orphan babies. We must take them under our wings at once!' She scooped up one of the eggs from a nearby crib and said 'I will love you if you are a gamalite or a dragon.' The other's followed suit and the nursery maid who had been so keen to get rid of the babies earlier was suddenly all maternal and kind as she looked out of the window to the back yard.

'There are more babies here!' she called to the others. 'Quickly, bring them all inside where they will be warm, and we can look after them properly.' They all then rushed outside and brought back the gamalites who stomped with small muddy feet about the nursery and adjoining playroom and were fussed over by the dragon attendants. The children thought how much kinder they must have been at one time before High Hat had brought them here to work as his staff. They couldn't wait to tell Manny and Griff – but right now they had to meet the others in the dining room.

It was like a busy train station down there crossed with a water fight, as Griff rushed around the edges of the room guiding a jug through the air and tipping it randomly over the crowd, determined that no one would be missed. Protesting students jostled for room and shouted about when they would be allowed home. Dragon kitchen assistants were circling above everyone's heads, flames shooting out of their mouths and nostrils, having ripped off their aprons and hats in protest.

They were all waiting for High Hat, who at any moment would certainly hear the din and put in an appearance. Manny was nowhere to be seen as Sabe and Megan searched the many faces in the crowds. They decided to check the empty kitchens where half-finished pies had been abandoned and saucepans were still full of raw vegetables. It was eerily quiet and on the floor in the centre lay Manny groaning and holding his head. He looked up as they came into the kitchen.

'I slipped over,' said Manny and he was clearly very worried. 'The floor just got so wet. We should have thought more carefully. I'm too old for this.' The children were afraid. *What if he died and none of them had any magic to save him?'* Megan instinctively crouched down next to Manny and held his hand. A strangely youthful hand for such an old man. Sabe looked closely at Manny who had stopped groaning.

'Megan look!' he said and pointed at Manny's face. 'Something is happening to Wizard Manny! I'll go and get Griff!'

High Hat stormed into the dining room and stood on the stage. He stamped his small feet and shouted for attention which was greeted with laughs and jeers. He looked panicked and shouted at Miss Hagworth and Miss Whizzity. 'Control them will you!'

The teachers smiled at him.

'Oh but we have. Only they have regained their memories and are off home shortly.' said Miss Hagworth.

'Well spray them with more Memory Breaker then!' he hissed at her. 'I cannot allow any sort of rebellion to get in the way of my plans.'

'We would,' said Miss Whizzity smugly. 'Only unfortunately it's all gone.' She looked towards the ceiling and nodded at the circling dragons who all swooped towards the little man on the stage knocking off his hat and grabbing his limbs in their mouths as they carried him away towards the ceiling. Everyone looked up at High Hat who was shouting and fighting to be freed from the dragon's grip. They circled the room with him, clearly enjoying his embarrassment, before stopping in the centre of the ceiling. There was a brief silence and the crowds of children instinctively moved to the sides of the room. The dragons let go of High Hat and down he fell, clumsily and landed with a thud on the floor as everyone looked on with a mixture of fascination and amusement. The two teachers strode up to him immediately. Miss Hagworth waved her wand in the air above him and a large net fell upon High Hat, pinning him to the spot.

'How dare you bring me here!' shouted Miss Whizzity. 'I had tickets for the Farsea Flower Show and now I have missed it! Take that!' she cried and smacked him with her clipboard.

'You dreadful little man!' cried Miss Hagworth. 'If I go home to find that my cake cupboards have been raided by those awful house-breaking goblins in my absence, trust me your scabby little feet will not touch the ground. I shall turn you into a peanut and put you out on my bird table!'

High Hat was getting more and more tangled up in the net as he tried to fight his way out of it. He looked up defiantly at the two women who stood over him.

'You were useless teachers anyway!' he shouted. 'I knew I should have taken on someone younger!'

'Come along Agnes' said Miss Whizzity linking arms with Miss Hagworth. 'Lets go and find a cafe and get a nice cup of tea and put the land to rights.' They turned and walked towards the door, turning back briefly to give High Hat a satisfied smile.

'Someone younger indeed!' said Miss Whizzity in disgust.

The crowd of students stepped back again, half afraid and half fascinated, to give the strange little man some space. By now, with the Memory Breaker Spell having worked on all of them, some had no idea who he was and a few of them felt that he was vaguely familiar. There was a long silence while everyone watched to see what would happen next.

High Hat stood up slowly in his net and dusted himself down. He looked angrily up at the ceiling where the dragons circled slowly, then at the crowds surrounding him. Marley stood at the side of the room and suddenly felt afraid. High Hat would surely turn them all into something not very pleasant...but instead he roared at the crowd of students.

'Out! Get out the lot of you! There is nothing to see here!'

'Well that's good,' shouted one of the students. 'Because we are all off home!'

A cheer went up from the crowd as they rushed excitedly to the door, calling to each other about how they couldn't wait to see their families. The dragons followed, flying downwards and landing on their feet as they then stomped dramatically to the door, breathing rebellious flames in High Hat's direction as they passed him by.

Soon the chatter of departing students grew faint and the dining hall was silent. There was just High Hat and Marley in the room staring intensely at each other.

Marley knew that this was his chance. He could feel himself shaking at the opportunity he now had, and he hoped High Hat couldn't see how nervous he was. *What now?* He should have been turned into a mouse or a frog by now surely? Yet as he looked down at the outfit he had chosen for himself that day in the market, he knew that he could make his own choices now, he needn't be scared and the realisation almost made him smile. High Hat was going no where for as long as that net held him down.

He knew that he could demand that High Hat to tell him the truth about why he had kept him hidden in the academy for so many years under the pretense that he was some up-and-coming great wizard. He could also demand that he leave him alone to live his life the way he chose to, far away from the academy. Alternatively there was the option of not saying anything and simply walking up to the dreadful little man and hitting him on the nose.

Marley, as it happened, felt strangely calm as he walked towards the man whom he was now sure he was not related to in any way. They stood looking at each other and Marley thought he saw High Hat shaking. Now was the time to get answers, but he stopped short. It no longer mattered.

'You're not worth it,' he muttered under his breath.

'Turn him into a miniature Marley!' shouted the familiar voice of Manny from the kitchen. Marley realised that Manny and Griff must have observed the whole thing.

'He's not worth it,' repeated Marley out loud. 'And I won't think of the past any more. I have a great life now and I'm going to enjoy it.'

'Marley,' called High Hat. 'I only wanted what was best for you. I knew that one day you would be one of the finest wizards this land had ever seen. You just needed time.'

'Who are you really?' asked Marley.

'I am High Hat! Your uncle and guardian, and I am the greatest wizard in the land. I have devoted my life to training people in magic.' Marley felt Sabe and Megan at his side and suddenly there was Griff too, holding one of the baby gamalites and stroking its head as he looked amused. Marley had to say something he had suspected for a long time.

'You're not my uncle and you're not a great wizard! You're not even a little bit wizard.

You don't actually have any magic do you?' High Hat looked lost for words and there was a silence once more.

'But we do!' said Manny from behind him.

High Hat looked up and his face fell.

'Hello again,' said Manny to High Hat and Marley could sense that he was enjoying the reaction he had stirred up.

Marley looked up at Manny who was no longer stooped and frail. It was still Wizard Manny, with his kind face and calm cheerful voice but he was now standing straight and strong, no longer confined by old age. Griff, Sabe and Megan stood next to the younger version of Manny, looking at him with pride and admiration.

'Come on now Marley, lets get you home,' he said and put his arm around him. 'It's Disappearing Spell time!' Then in a puff of green smoke they were all gone.

The Reunion

Back at the palace, Queen Augustine was flitting between intense impatience and tearful desperation.

'I can't believe you are refusing to help me!' she shouted at Amy. 'I am the queen! You must not disobey my orders!' The next minute tears would start to fall, and she looked like a confused and lonely child.

'I need my family back,' she sobbed 'I miss my family, I will do anything please.' Amy was one moment trying to hold and comfort her and the next jumping away from her in fear of what threats she might come out with next. She too was longing to go home by this stage.

'Anyone for seconds?' called Ben as he held up a tray of desserts in fake enthusiasm and made a move towards the door.

'No!' shouted the queen and Amy simultaneously. Ben reluctantly sat back down and wondered if anyone would notice if he took his phone off the table and put it back in his pocket while the girls were arguing. It was okay for Luna. She hated dramatic scenes so had made an exit some time ago to look for Tip before the queen noticed what an extra guest was doing there.

The green smoke cloud that suddenly appeared in the dining room made everyone cough. Five...no six... people suddenly appeared! There was Sabe and Megan looking pleased with themselves, Marley was looking relieved. *What on earth was High Hat doing trapped in a net like a prize crab and who was the young man with Griff?* The atmosphere was pierced by a cry of joy from Queen Augustine.

'Daddy! Dad!' she shouted in delight and rushed forwards to the younger Manny and Griff who both embraced her immediately. Manny buried his face in the queen's hair.'

'Hello my darling,' he said. 'We've missed you.'

Queen Augustine began to cry and turned to Amy and mouthed. 'Thank you.'

'Does anyone want to let us know what is going on?' said Ben as he quickly retrieved his phone.

'This is my daddy King Emmanuel,' said Queen Augustine. 'Better known as Manny, and this is my dad Griff.'

Sabe and Megan looked at each other in surprise. 'Two dads?' they whispered to each other. Had they heard right?

'Yes two dads,' laughed Queen Augustine. 'What's so strange about that?'

'Nothing' said Sabe. 'We just assumed...well I guess we should have learned by now not to assume anything! I'm happy for you.'

'He looks good doesn't he?' said Megan nodding in Manny's direction. Amy squinted. It was Manny but he looked so young.

'Have you had plastic surgery, Manny?' asked Ben and Amy sighed. Brothers were so annoying sometimes.

'I've been under a spell for a long time,' explained Manny. 'I thought I was an old wizard, I couldn't remember a time that I didn't live in Holiday Land where Griff and I ran the sanctuary together. When I slipped on Memory Breaker, the spell was broken. We both remembered who we were and we came back home to find you.'

'High Hat did it,' said Griff. 'He split up our family to stop our magic working, and now he has a lot of explaining to do, don't you my dear old friend.' Everyone turned to look at High Hat, who had lost his hat and shoes in the scuffle with the dragons and who wasn't looking at all like his name.

'So he is Marley's uncle then?' said Sabe.

'Not exactly,' said Queen Augustine 'He's an old friend of my parents. He was born magic and trained to be a wizard with dad, but he wasn't very good at it, actually that's an understatement, he was useless at it, but he had a good brain and could memorise any spell. He was destined to be a great teacher.'

'High Hat was also good at organising. Something that is so important when you have a kingdom to run,' said Manny. 'We felt sorry for him when he could never progress as a wizard as he was a good friend of ours, but we trusted him and knew he had other skills so eventually he became our chief advisor to the palace and a guardian to our girls.'

'He did a wonderful job,' continued Griff. 'But as his influence grew we did suspect he was becoming greedy, both for power and riches. We found out that he was forming secret alliances with other magical people in the land. He wanted what he couldn't have.'

'In more ways than one,' said Queen Augustine.

'Your sister?' remembered Sabe. 'He told me when we were at the academy. He loved the eldest princess but she fell in love with someone else.' Griff and Manny exchanged knowing glances.

'Frank?' said Megan.

'She loved me,' interrupted High Hat from under the net. 'Until he came along and ruined everything.' he looked at

Marley as he said the name.

'Me?' said Marley. 'It couldn't have been me. I would have remembered if I had ever been to this palace or known the princesses.

Ben suddenly thought of the photo in his pocket and handed it round. Manny and Griff nodded as they recognised the person in it.

'That's definitely Frank,' they agreed.

Marley was handed the photo once more and he studied it closely. It did seem to make sense although something in the back of his head was telling him there was more to this story. The child in the photo looked just like him, yet he felt instinctively it wasn't.

'So, you punished me by taking me away to the academy and wiping my memory because you wanted my girlfriend? Even if that were true you can't have thought it was going to be a long-term thing. I don't care for girls, not in that way, and even if I did it's a bit over the top to do what you did. So my real name is Frank then?' he looked thoughtful. Manny and Griff were nodding. Queen Augustine looked uncomfortable.

'No your name is Marley,' she said. She went to sit back at the dining table and motioned for everyone else to do the same. She looked deep in thought.

'It all makes sense now,' she said sadly. 'You see Frank was our childhood friend and he would visit us often from the time he accidentally stumbled upon our land. He more or less grew up with us and was often at the palace. But Marley is not the same person as Frank. Marley is from our land and he was born here.' She looked at Manny and Griff who were shaking their heads.

'You've had a lot to take in today darling,' said Griff as he took her hand reassuringly. 'It's bound to be confusing for you. I mean, it has been over a hundred years since Frank disappeared. Don't feel pressured to come up with answers.'

Queen Augustine looked at Griff and then at Manny and she didn't look at all confused. She then looked at Marley again who was still studying the photo and trying to make sense of things.

High Hat's voice boomed from under his net in the corner of the room where he was now curled up and looking defeated.

'You might as well tell your parents the truth Augustine!' he shouted. 'About how you and your sisters conspired to dilute the pure bloodline!'

'What?' said Manny. Queen Augustine took a deep breath.

'Marley you were born here. I should know, I was there when you arrived. My sisters and I decided to raise you in secret as we desperately wanted you, especially my older sister. She was distraught after Frank disappeared. You were all she had left of him you see. You belonged to her and Frank, but you were never going to be a pure blood wizard and so we created The Land of Childhood to hide you in when we needed to.'

'But why didn't you tell us?' said Manny. 'We wouldn't have been angry. We adored Frank too. You can't help who you love.'

'Humph!' interrupted High Hat. 'Exactly. I was in love with the eldest princess! She was mine. Frank ruined everything as soon as he grew up and then she only had eyes for him. A great husband he would have been. He disappeared without a trace over a hundred years ago, after some pathetic excuse about having duty to do in his own world. She could have had a future with me but oh no! Marley had to arrive and mess that plan up too!'

'Anyone for seconds?' asked Ben.

'No!' shouted everyone at once before Megan added. 'Well maybe I could manage a small dessert,' but Ben was prevented from leaving the room so she resigned herself to waiting a while longer.

'So let's get this right,' said Sabe. 'Frank was a boy from our world who accidentally discovered this kingdom, like we did but over a hundred years ago.'

'That's right,' said Queen Augustine. 'He came to visit for years and he was a wonderful friend. He used to visit until he grew up. Eventually he and my elder sister fell in love but they didn't think their love would ever be accepted as he wasn't like us. You see our sister was expected to marry a wizard like herself.'

'So Marley was their baby!' said Megan. Marley sat very quietly, taking it all in. It was starting to make sense slowly. So he wasn't a gamalite after all.

'He was a secret,' said Queen Augustine. 'Only Frank never knew about Marley, as he disappeared one day and never came back to visit again.'

'Why not?' said Megan.

'We don't know,' said Queen Augustine.

Ben looked up.

'The First World War of course!' he remarked. 'The timings make sense. In our world,' he explained to the others, 'there was a big war. Frank would have had to go and fight and I don't think he could come back!'

'No he just didn't want Marley!' interrupted High Hat.

'I don't believe you!' shouted Marley back at him and went to give Augustine a hug.

'I wish I could remember,' he said.

The door opened and in came Luna, casually at first without a care in the world. Then she saw Manny and Griff and shouted excitedly, 'Daddy! Dad! Where have you been? I found Frank but he's called Marley now and Augustine has turned into a bossy boots!' She rushed up to them and Griff picked her up and kissed her on the cheek. Augustine looked a little offended but then she smiled and remembered her sister's humour. She hugged Luna.

'Hello our Little Princess, where have *you* been?'

'At the cottage with Marley and his blue cat of course!' she said to her parents as if she'd only been out for the afternoon. 'You'll meet her later, she's Marley's familiar. She's being spoiled in the kitchen with all the leftovers.'

The children looked at the family and it felt good to see them reunited and knowing they had played a part in it – but there seemed to be a few questions left to answer.

'Memory Breaker!' said Sabe suddenly. 'Has anyone got any of the spell left? If Marley has some then he will remember when he lived here.'

'And if Amy has some maybe she will remember her powers and use some of them to bring back my other sister,' said Queen Augustine enthusiastically.

Everyone turned out their pockets. Griff had half a water pistol left and he handed it to Marley.

'It doesn't seem right to fire this at you,' he said. 'You can drink some if you want.'

Marley took the water pistol off Griff and squirted some Memory Breaker into his mouth. He then handed it to Amy who looked dubious before doing the same. Everyone waited to see what would happen next.

'Nothing' said Marley after a few minutes. 'I only remember

being at the academy.'

'Nothing,' said Amy. 'Except for some summer holiday homework I totally forgot to start.'

'Well that's that then' shrugged Marley 'I will never know my parents.'

Queen Augustine started to speak 'But you are one of us.'

'You're family,' said Manny. 'I knew there was something special about you. I felt it as soon as we met. The only other time I have ever felt a bond like that was with Little One my dragon familiar. That's why I knew I could trust you with her after I have gone.'

Marley looked up quickly.

'Little One? You mean the dragon that turned into Luna?'

Manny and Griff looked like they were about to cry. They turned on High Hat who was still trying to justify his behaviour from under his net in the corner.

'You turned our youngest daughter into a dragon!' shouted Manny in disbelief.

'You stopped Frank coming back to the land forever!' shouted Griff.

'I swear I did nothing to Frank,' piped up High Hat. 'I wanted to, but I just couldn't do it. You're right I was jealous, but one day it was like all my wishes had been granted and he said something about doing some sort of duty and he would be back soon. Then he just disappeared and never came back.'

For Marley, the pieces were falling into place. He noticed Tip quietly enter the room and he picked her up. All he needed right now was a cuddle from his best blue friend. Tip nuzzled against his face.

'She should have told us,' said Manny 'We would have been

upset at first of course but we could have helped her and Frank. She didn't need to hide Marley. I can't believe we never knew.'

'High Hat found out about Marley and he was very angry,' said Queen Augustine.

High Hat roared and grappled with his net. 'The kingdom would have been ruined forever! The magic would have been weakened. Do you realise that Marley was heir to the throne! A half human with no magic, ruling a magical kingdom like this. I had to do what I did to protect the future of our land!' He then turned to Queen Augustine 'You threatened to tell your parents the truth, and that's when I knew I had to do something fast. I had to erase all your memories and split up your family to be extra sure that none of your would remember a thing or find each other. I think I did it in quite a decent way though. I made sure young Luna stayed with her parents.'

'You made us age like common wizards and mortals!' shouted Manny. 'We forgot that we had three daughters. You robbed us of our family!'

'Well you had a nice retirement in Holiday Land didn't you?' said High Hat, quickly. 'Marley got an education with me, much better for him than playing all day long and being spoiled by his mother and aunts. I made sure Queen Augustine had everything she would ever need, palaces, fine clothes.'

'But I was so lonely!' shouted Augustine. 'I needed my family.'

'I should have had my family too' said Marley sadly.

'And what did you do with your favourite sister? The one you loved but who wouldn't love you back?' asked Sabe.

'Oh that was easy,' replied High Hat. 'I punished her...I turned her into a cat.'

There was a silence as everyone tried to take in what High Hat had just revealed. The missing sister! The missing piece of the puzzle, Marley's real mother, who had been punished by High Hat for falling in love with a human, had all along been living a secret life as a cat.

'Tip?' said Marley softly as he looked at Tip who was fading into dust before his eyes. High Hat put his head in his hands and let out a load defeatist groan. The dust, which a moment ago had been Tip, fell to the floor and a silver mist began to rise and grow and take on a familiar outline.

'Tippi!' shouted Queen Augustine as she recognised the figure of a tall raven-haired young woman with kind brown eyes, eyes that looked remarkably like Marley's.

Luna suddenly piped up,

'Tippi been away! Has she brought me a present back?'

Tip, or rather Tippi, crouched down to Luna's level and said to her,

'Yes Luna, I have brought you a present.' She looked at Marley and extended her hand 'Marley who we both love so much is your uncle, my son. I have been away for many long years secretly searching for him and longing to find him and never let him go again. Now I have found him, and we are going to be a family again.'

Luna looked behind her at where Marley was standing quite still and wondering if the events unfolding before him were actually happening. He had longed for a family but now he had one, the best family ever, he didn't know how to act or what to say. He wanted to hug Tip but he was so used to picking her up when she had been in cat form he didn't know what to do with her now.'

'You're so, so erm, lady... er... mum like,' he said quietly and looked at the children for guidance. They motioned for him to go and hug her, but Marley stood still, frozen in disbelief to the spot. Luna started to laugh.

'Silly Marley! His face is all red and wet like a strawberry in the rain!' she observed.

The announcement brought Marley back to the moment.

'I'll give you silly Marley!' he laughed and started to chase Luna around the dining table pretending to roar as she squealed in delight.

'Nothing's changed there then,' smiled Tip. 'He needs some time, and we have plenty. Come on let's go and celebrate. Land of Childhood anyone?'

Everyone agreed enthusiastically and got ready to leave the room.

'Excuse me everyone,' said Ben. 'Aren't you forgetting something?' He pointed at High Hat who was crouched in the corner muttering angrily to himself and still trying to get out of his net where the magic held it still over him.

'Oh he'll be fine where he is for a few hours,' said Manny. 'And don't worry I have a plan for what to do with him.'

So they all left the room, parading proudly through the corridors as the palace staff gasped in amazement before darting off to spread the news.

'King Emmanuel is back!' they called to everyone who would hear them. 'King Griffin is home! And the Princesses Tippi, Augustine and Luna! Come and see! Come and see!'

'And Prince Marley,' said Tip. 'Our new member of the family. Wait until we introduce him! Everyone will be so excited.'

The group ran, skipped and chattered along into the garden and through the maze as the palace gardeners downed their tools and pointed in astonishment at the family who had returned and the vivid colours of the newly blooming trees and flowers.

'It's the combined magic of the family that has made this happen!' remarked Amy. 'So it must have been Luna and Marley's return to the palace that started the magic and made the flowers bloom and broken things start to work again. I'm glad it wasn't me. I was getting worried.'

They climbed into the fountain, one by one, and emerged in the Land of Childhood where they celebrated with a great picnic of treats which Marley and the children brought back from the village shops. They then took the train into the village square and chose each other gifts. Luna finally got a unicorn which she rode happily about on, Marley got a real racing car from Tip which he took her for a spin in, or rather a slow drive around to remember all the attractions she had created for him all those years ago. He had to endure a talking to about not going to fast but when he got back, he winked at the children and told them once her back was turned, he was going to see just how fast he could really go!

Manny and Griff talked excitedly about how they were going to move into the academy with Luna and create a wonderful home for all the rescued gamalites and spent the afternoon choosing furniture and brightly-coloured paint to brighten up what they called the drab and dingy interior. Their two eldest daughters were old enough now, they explained,to run the kingdom from the palace and they would help when needed. High Hat, they revealed would be the sanctuary maid until he learned his lesson, for as long as that took.

'He will be held there by powerful magic,' explained Griff. 'He will never be able to leave until he is ready to change his ways. He will be a servant to both us and the gamalites and will spend his days changing their litter trays, cleaning up and singing them to sleep.' Everyone agreed that it sounded like a hard job but a fair punishment.

'But where are you going to live Marley?' asked Sabe.

'I'm going to live with Tip of course!' said Marley excitedly, 'And Luna will come and stay whenever she likes.' He decided to ask Tip something.

'Mother, now that we have more space can I have a dragon?'

Tip rolled her eyes and said, 'I suppose so, as long as it stays on the ground floor, those palace ceilings are very expensive to fix if we get a dragon jumping on them!'

The children were so tired that evening as they floated down the Rainbow River in a large open topped boat with the firefly lanterns twinkling above their heads and they told the rabbit captain all about what had happened. They each carried their own bags of toys and games that they had gifted to each other from the Land of Childhood, and they were looking forward to spending the last few days of the summer holidays playing with them in the house.

As they passed by each platform, they could see that the news of the family's return had spread fast. Little people and animals were busy swarming about, hanging up bunting and fairy lights around their houses and bringing out tiny tables and chairs ready for street parties. They passed by some gardens that backed onto the river where Megan had been told off for helping herself to a garden path made of boiled sweets. They could see some gnome builders digging up the paths and removing the sweet paving slabs into a skip. Megan stood up at once and waved at the builders.

'Excuse me, what are you doing with those paving slabs?' A

gnome that was busy carrying a large boiled sweet on his back stopped and looked at Megan.

'Kings orders! The whole land is going to be spruced up and put back to how it used to be. We are laying a new path.'

'Ooh' said Megan excitedly. 'Do you mind if I have that then?' Her eyes grew wide as she observed the giant red sweet.

'Help yourself' shrugged the gnome and carried the sweet towards the boat where he passed it to Megan. She sat and looked at in delight as it took up all the space on her lap.

'You are never going to eat all that!' said Ben.

'Of course not! I'm taking this into school with me as a souvenir for all my friends,' she said proudly, imagining her classmates' faces as she carried the bright red boulder into school.

They reached the orchard platform and waved goodbye to the rabbit.

'Come back soon,' he told them as they carried their bags towards the rope swings that led up to the orchard. It took a while to get up with all the bags and the giant sweet but eventually they managed it and climbed up into the orchard.

It was raining again, and the grass was deep green and high and the bright flowers bowed their heads so much under the weight of the rain that the children could just about make out the odd fairy sheltering inside and waving to them.

It would be autumn soon and the hot sunny days were going to become fewer. The summer holidays were drawing to a close and the new school year beckoned. Whatever adventures awaited them there nothing was going to come close to the summer they had all had!

By the time they reached the back door of the house they were soaked and muddy. Sabe's mother, who had been waiting for them flung open the door.

'We've been wondering where you have been! We were about to send out a search party!'

She helped them take off their wet shoes and socks and called to their father to bring down some towels. She couldn't get over the size of the boiled sweet Megan told her she had bought in the town. Mr Williams, now a frequent visitor to their kitchen was sitting at the table, his round tummy touching the side of it as he was finishing off yet another plate of whatever their mother had made for him. Ben nudged Megan.

'See that's going to be you in a few years,' and she smacked him playfully on his arm.

'I'll make you all something on toast. You must be so hungry!' said their mother. The children exchanged looks of horror.

'Actually would you mind if we had something else? Fruit or soup or something like that?' His mother looked surprised.

'Well okay if that's what you prefer' and she went to open the fridge.

Ben walked up to Mr Williams.

'Hello Mr Williams' he said and held out the black and white photo of Frank. 'I borrowed this photo of your grandfather. I hope you don't mind, you see he looks so much like a friend of ours I wanted to show him. I wish I could have met him. It's a shame he died in the war.'

Mr Williams took the photo off Ben and placed it back carefully inside his pocket. He looked puzzled as he stared at the children.

'Died?' he said. 'Whoever told you he died? Of course he

didn't die! He came back from the war you know.' The children looked at one another. They couldn't believe it.

'But what happened to him? You said you never met him?' said Amy 'Oh I didn't,' said Mr Williams and beckoned them close and whispered. 'He disappeared soon after he came back.' he then nodded at them.

'But how?' asked Sabe 'what happened to him?'

'Well that' said Mr Williams 'Is a bit of a mystery, but I think we should save it for another day don't you?'